FOUND

GARGOYLES DEN BOOK THREE

I0562153

Lisa Barry

𝔚itching 𝔥our 𝔓ublishing Inc.

Found is a fictional work. The characters, places, and events portrayed in this book are from the imagination of the author or are used fictitiously. Any similarity to real persons, living or dead, business establishments, events or locales is entirely coincidental and not intended by the authors. The publisher does not have any control over and does not assume any responsibility for the author or any third party websites or publications or their content.

Witching Hour Publishing, Inc.

ISBN-13: 978-1-943121-63-2

Editor: Courtenay Dodds www.CourtenayDodds.com

Cover Creator: https://www.facebook.com/ammonia.nikolova

For Rhi and Court.

Thank you for always believing in me.

My Music Muse

Music is definitely my muse and when I have any issues getting out the words that build this wonderful world, I listen for the inspiration I need.

I can be inspired by any manner of music types. I like everything from classical to punk to old school alternative to 70's easy listening. My main love is whatever you want to call the genre which includes Chevelle, Red, Korn, Static-X, Disturbed, etc. The only style I just cannot get into is country. My friend Rhi says that one day she will find a country song for me. I doubt it but I'll entertain her. :)

This book was different than the first two for me. After the events of Book Two, I found a restlessness with this book. The way it was supposed to go just wasn't going. Finally, I remembered to plug into the music and the words came. They didn't follow the outline, they hard rebelled against going the way I had planned, and the story ended up concluding SO MUCH better than the original outline.

If you go to YouTube and look up epic music play lists, this is the style of playlist on my Pandora station and what I listened to for most of this book. There is one scene, the first scene with Sloane in the forest that came directly from listening to Jennifer Thomas' *Rainforest*. I was driving home from work one day playing Jennifer's lovely album *Illumination* and the song brought me straight to the forest. I actually teared up as I watched the scene play out in my mind. (Don't worry, I kept an eye on the road too.)

I hope you enjoy this book and I hope you love how everything wraps up as much as I did.

Also, if I have recommended any music that moved you, let me know!

~~ When we are lost, may we all be FOUND. ~~

Lisa Barry

ACKNOWLEDGMENTS

There are three people in my life that I want to call out. They support the shit out of me and I want them to really know how amazing they are and how much their love and care means to me.

Rhiannon always has time to hear an idea, read a chapter or run through a problem. She gives fantastic feedback and always has a smile to brighten the day. Plus we are co-writing an EPIC story together which is so FUN and I can't wait to get it done and share it.

Courtenay always reminds me of the bright side, the things I've completed, the words I've written and ALL the right things that are good. Plus she made me a gargoyle cake for my birthday. Best ever! Lastly, she's my editor so she helps make my words shiny and sparkly.

Kimbo is not only my best friend, my soul mate, the father to my children but he's my biggest fan. He manages to make me feel like the most talented and incredible writer in the whole world. And he's nice to look at, so there's that.

There are many others who shine light on my life regularly; my brother and his funny sense of humor, my sister-in-law with her care for detail, my mom and step-dad who take care of us so well even when we're far away, my daughter is my biggest cheerleader and my son's focus drives me to better my discipline (I love them both so much!), my writer's group (the Ink Slingers Guild: www.InkSlingersGuild.com) helps keep my mind keen and my words flowing, and lastly but not leastly, the Facebook group for authors, 20Books. Though I still have so much to learn, their vast well of knowledge has been incredibly helpful and encouraging.

I thank you all from the bottom, top and sides of my heart.

Chapter 1

Helen Barrows, Queen of the Guardians, barely glanced at the long scar down her right leg as she dressed in one of her many suits as she prepared to head to the office. She knew she was not required to wear a suit to brief the teachers at the Guardian School but she found them comfortable. It helped her to set apart and differentiate between Queen work, school work, and play. Today's brief was of the Queen variety.

She debated the decisions she'd made and the courses of action she was taking, thus the cause for the staff brief.

She would be putting people in danger, again. It was the nature of her life. A life which had taken a turn recently and loss was more of a concern than in the past. Previously the only deaths she'd had to worry about were due to age or the rare deadly injury, more often from general living than being sent out to protect the masses. The Guardians were virtually indestructible.

Her mind turned briefly to the scar on her leg. She saw it every day but rarely gave it any thought. For some reason her mind kept redirecting today.

The scar made her think of Marten, and she

didn't want to think about him. Not for a minute or a second. He was dead to her and she had made sure everyone else who'd known him had stopped mentioning that he ever was. It was childish she supposed as she slid a foot into a flesh colored high heel.

The Director, her husband walked into the bedroom to collect her. She put on her other shoe and stood. He gave her the soft smile that had melted her heart so many years ago and she calmed, returning his smile with a similar one of her own.

"I think you're doing the right thing, love," he commented as he came to stand before her. He placed a hand on her cheek, and she leaned into it. She didn't need his approval, but she loved his support. Helen felt incredibly lucky to have found him when she young. They were able to shape each other over the years and fall into a happy companionship that helped her through many tough decisions.

"I've been thinking of him again," she confessed. Joseph Barrows was the only person in the world who would know who she meant.

"I wonder what he's up to," he said.

"I fear the answer," she fretted. He pulled her into a hug.

"We can't help them all," he whispered into her hair. She sighed and took in his strength. She liked how he said 'we', but she knew it was just *her* who carried the burden. At least with him by her side, the burden was easier to bare.

Time to get to it. She straightened and they

pulled out of the hug though his hand lingered on her lower back as they left room.

Chapter 2

Lauren, more commonly known as El, paused when she rounded the corner of the underground prison she called home. Jacob sat in his usual spot at the end of the dirt packed hallway but today he was more hunched than usual. The tube running from his arm and into the sorry excuse for a ceiling was the likely culprit. She'd seen so many of his kind die at the hand of her captor, but Jacob was special. He had wiggled his way into her heart with kindness and terrible jokes despite the fact his life was being bled from him a little every day.

Because of her.

His death was imminent because she had been born. He was there for the sole purpose of hiding her from the rest of the world.

She hated it.

Lauren continued down the hall. When she reached him, Jacob blinked his eyes open and focused. He smiled in spite of his condition.

"Hey, El." He sounded like he had cotton in his mouth.

Lauren fought the tears. She didn't want to show weakness to him, or to anyone.

"Hey, slacker," she said instead and placed the checkerboard onto the table next to him. She sat in the other chair and proceeded to put out the playing pieces. She glanced up to see Jacob's eyes had fluttered shut. His breathing was labored. Lauren blinked before shooting up from the chair. She grabbed the pieces she had already put out and shoved them and the board back into her bag.

"Sorry, Jacob." She gently touched his arm. "I totally forgot I left something in my room. Back in a few."

He barely moved in answer, just a shift in his lips and the tiniest of smiles. Lauren ran back down the hall and as soon as she rounded the corner, flattened her back against the wall. She gulped in air as tears rush down her face. She couldn't do it. She just couldn't face his end. Lauren cried quietly as the cool dirt packed wall seeped a chill into her spine. Time passed by in tears, heartbeats, and silent wails. Leaving her bag on the ground, she peered around the corner. He was fully slumped down now. She approached Jacob carefully, watching for a rise in his chest or a motion of a hand but, as she had expected, there was nothing.

Sitting down on the ground at his feet, she curled herself around one of his legs and placed her head on his knee and cried again. No matter how many friends she lost this way, the pain always wrapped itself around her and squeezed. There was no end to their misery.

Or hers.

Chapter 3

Helen paced the command center room while throwing out her magic as far as she could reach. Her husband worked nearby, tirelessly scanning all of the communication devices for any news. Periodically he would move to her, take her hands and give whatever magic and strength he could to their bond so she could add to her own.

Waiting was always the hardest part.

A pulse struck from out of the blue and stabbed through her core. The Queen leaned heavily on the nearest wall. Her throat allowed only a fraction of air through as the fear and pain of a lost guardian rushed into her heart. Her nerves screamed and her blood slowed.

Joseph appeared before her.

"What is it, Helen?" he asked, his voice commanding and urgent.

"I've lost another," she whispered back.

FOUND

Chapter 4

"What's wrong with her?" Verity asked. She stared at the woman, her shoulders bent and her arms hanging at her sides. There was no way out of this, and she knew it. When Duran had rushed ahead of her friends in the Faeways and then kidnapped her and brought her here, the little bit of trust she'd given him had vanished like a puff of smoke. The strange spatial travel of the Fae had left a sour taste in her mouth and a wobble in her stance, but Verity couldn't ignore the sick woman in front of her.

She had no way of knowing who and what this person was or what was wrong without touching her. The aftermath of the jump had left her feeling off kilter. Her skin crawled and her ears itched. She had experienced these same effects when they were in the Faeways although not as acutely.

Getting near the lady would mean getting close to him. He was on her shit list like nobody's business. *How dare he?* First, he was simply a jerk, then he had claimed her in front of other Fae folk - supposedly for her own protection. Now he wanted her to be a nurse for him? Her nerves started jumping and zinging. She clenched her fists waiting for his answer.

Fix her he had ordered the moment they had appeared in the room, just after he'd taken her away from her friends as if that hadn't already bristled her tender nerves.

"If I knew that, Verity, dear, I could handle her myself, now couldn't I?" Duran knelt next to the large bed and held the sickly white hand in his own. The girl's age was hard to read. She seemed very young, in her late teens by Verity's standards, but in the Fae world, Verity didn't know what things to look for in order to gauge the age. The girl's skin was so pale Verity could make out greenish veins moving slowly beneath. Her breathing was soft and slow.

"What makes you think that I will have a clue?"

He stood fluidly, startling Verity to step back. She hit a something and turned to steady herself on the small table. It was then she noticed the room was floral in both design and decoration. The scent of mixed flowers was part of what was making Verity feel a bit queasy. It was too much.

Before Duran could answer her, she waved a hand in the air. "The first thing you can do is get some fresh air in here."

"She loves flowers," he said.

"So do I." Verity crossed the few steps and sat on the edge of the bed. "But I don't want to drown in them."

In moments, the room smelled like a fresh meadow with the softest breeze in the air.

"That's much better."

Duran leaned against the wall and folded his arms across his broad chest. Verity put her hand on the girl's forehead. It was lukewarm at best.

"What's her name?"

"Lerina," he answered softly.

"And how long has she been this way?"

"Sixteen years."

Verity's whipped her head around to meet his eyes. "What?"

He shrugged.

"Do you know what happened sixteen years ago?" It seemed like such a long time to be on the brink of death.

"I found her this way." Duran voice was stronger now.

Verity sighed loudly before pressing her lips together. Getting information from Duran could take all day. Or night. She was never sure what was up or down with him.

She leaned over Lerina and put her hands gently on the girl's clavicle. Verity let her hands accustom to the temperature, the dryness of the skin, and slightest beat of her heart. Pushing gently down, Verity let her magic, for lack of a better word, slip from her hands and into the Fae woman.

A painful shock registered on her palms and Verity pulled away with a screech.

"Damn it!" Duran bellowed and stalked around the room shaking his fisted hands.

Shaking out her own hands, Verity understood.

"So, you were hoping I could break through whatever is holding her like this."

"I had hoped." He let his head drop and rubbed

his forehead.

"Well, I'm not sure how I'm going to do much better. You have lord knows how many more years of experience than me."

Duran turned to her and stopped. He cocked his head like he was listening for something then rolled his eyes. A moment later Rothald, his brother, appeared in the room. Rothald wasn't his real name, none of the Fae would never share that, but it was what he'd told Verity she could call him if she ever needed him.

Verity frowned when she realized she should have called him for help and had completely forgotten she could. She recalled his innocence as a child and almost smiled. Looking at him now, one would never believe she had rescued him as a young Fae trapped in the underground prison of a madman. The Fae aged differently she'd learned, or rather time passed differently in the Faelands. The last time she had seen him, he'd told her to just call his name if she ever needed his assistance. Considering he was here now and not alarmed, Verity decided she wouldn't sound any alarms just yet even though she was still ruffled by Duran's actions. He seemed so human and then he would do something that reminded her he was not even close.

"My dear, Verity," Rothald said and dipped slightly as he took one of her hands in his own. "I am delighted you have come to visit." Verity glanced at Duran.

"It wasn't exactly planned," she told him dryly but smiled for the one she considered the good brother.

"Oh dear. Well, I am glad to have you just the same!" He moved to the bed and looked aloofly at the sleeping, or whatever was happening with her, lady.

"I take it you have not been able to help our Lerina?"

"I'm afraid not. Whatever ails her is not letting me get close."

Rothald hummed for a moment before turning to Verity once more.

"We are having a feast tonight. It is the last in the celebration of my coming of age. Would you accompany me as my esteemed guest?"

Verity blinked. Duran snorted in derision. Rothald smiled. Verity started to wonder what exactly was wrong with these...she thought people, but they weren't people, were they?

Their strangeness was confusing, and Verity wasn't sure what was a facade or not. She smiled at Rothald. When in Rome.

"That would be lovely! But I don't have anything appropriate to wear."

"That," Duran interrupted, "is the least of your worries."

Verity recalled when Duran had supposedly claimed her in front of another Fae. She frowned again. Her skin tickled and the oddest zing crept up her spine and out the top of her head. She wondered if there was a drug in the air or something about the Fae dimension she was allergic to. Her stomach turned slightly before righting itself.

"We shall provide you with something remarkable to wear, my dear. There is much beauty to enjoy, here in our lands."

"Sounds marvelous, Rothald. Lead the way."

She took Rothald's proffered arm and headed toward a door in the corner she hadn't seen before. She was pretty sure it had not been there before. As they walked through, she turned back to see Duran sink down onto the bed and take Lerina's hand in his own again. He looked so sad.

The faint smell of flowers and the light ocean breeze ended abruptly. Verity found her senses filled with a faint but sweet and overwhelmingly desirable odor.

"What is that?" she inquired dreamily, blinking herself into awareness.

Rothald appeared amused. "It's just the way our land."

Verity shook her head at his answer and continued with her stroll to meet the Queen.

FOUND

Chapter 5

The sound of wolves somewhere in the distance struck Sloan as odd seeing as how wolves were not known to be in this particular area. It was a humid but tolerable day and of all things, Sloane was taking a walk in a nearby bird sanctuary. To clear her head of conversations and feelings, it was an effort to have some general peace. Liam was out with Kam helping a friend remodel their home and she had a few hours to herself.

Maybe they weren't wolves. Sloane was no expert but whatever was filling the air with their wild calls, it was like a beat of music to her ears. She listened intently as she meandered the rarely used trail. A peacock sounded off from somewhere in a tree and several more echoed their annoyance at the invasion of their home. Sloane swatted a mosquito away as she picked up the soft gurgle of a small creek hidden by heavy bushes laden with some red berry even the birds wouldn't eat.

A woodpecker became busy, the mesmerizing tick-tick-tick sound echoing off through the trees as he searched for dinner. A chittering noise burst out and two young squirrels ran across the trail and vanished behind. Sloane smiled in memory of Bob, her Brownie friend who showed himself in the form of a squirrel. She hadn't seen him lately but was pretty sure he kept an eye on her still.

Sloane stopped and closed her eyes. The sounds of the forest crept into her skin, the life seeping into her muscles and filled her heart. Sloane felt the overwhelming desire to dance.

And so she did.

Her hands fluttered in the air while her feet moved so elegantly, she would not have recognized herself.

The leaves crunched beneath her feet, and the forest filled her senses. The thoughts and feelings of the creatures started to pour into her mind. Curiosity, fear, happiness, loneliness, anger, and love. The song in Sloane's mind played and played and played. She opened her eyes briefly and saw them, the animals of this particular place who had come to see the Aspie in their mist. There was a deer, two skunks, more squirrels and rabbits than she could count, the woodpecker she'd heard earlier, several peacocks who eyed her skeptically while a little gray fox watched with a sly smile on its face. Realizing the howls she had heard earlier were likely shape shifters perked the corners of Sloane's lips.

The song of the forest became more silent as the animals dropped what they were doing to visit her. Sloane stopped dancing then and crouched down. Some of the rabbits, a squirrel and the fox came to sniff her outstretched hand. One of the skunks licked it before scrunching up its nose.

Sloane could feel their thoughts, knew their challenges, and feel their interest in her. The bond with Liam was helping her powers to surface and then settle into her bones like a fond memory.

She opened up her senses further, determined to test her strength.

A faint tendril of dark fear slid into her neck and Sloane stood abruptly. The magic ended with a slam of horror. The animals fled and soon just the fox stood half hidden, watching from the safety of a thorn covered bush.

Closing her eyes, Sloane pushed her mind out in the direction of the fear that had licked her awareness. As soon as she had a good general idea, she started to run.

Her phone buzzed in her pocket as she sped through the trees. She didn't stop but pulled it out as she ran and hit the answer key.

"What's wrong, love?" She heard Liam's deep voice.

"Another child," she forced out.

"I'm coming."

Chapter 6

"He's one of the Lumin, a distant cousin to the Goblins," the Queen said as she stood with her back to them and gazed out the window. She was referring to the creature that had attempted to kidnap Andy. After arriving at the airport, he had jumped into the school's vehicle to head in and restart his classes only to find a new driver at the wheel. Super creepy, glowing skin and eyes so light, they were almost white. A chill ran down Andy's spine just thinking about him. He was sure that had nothing to do with the fact the guy had tried to kidnap him and when that didn't work, had tried to run him down in the school's classic car.

"Lumin." Keppin tasted the word. It fit the strange, pale man.

Andy and Keppin took up the seats in front of the Queen's desk as her husband, the Director, stood near the door, cell phone in hand. Keppin raised a brow at Andy, who shook head.

"They tend to rent themselves out for jobs," the Director said, "and get a payday with no real interest in the questionable morality of the job they've taken."

"Aren't we trained to do that?" Keppin asked

without thinking. The Queen turned and ice blue eyes landed on him.

"We have high integrity and strong moral fiber," she told him flatly. The Director cleared his throat and Keppin pressed his lips together. Andy tried not to smile.

"Why would anyone want me?" he asked.

"That is a good question," the Director answered.

"Because you're a displacer," the Queen stated. She sat at her desk and Andy could see the weariness in the fall of her shoulders and the faded blue lines under her eyes. He wanted to do anything to help alleviate her stress and he guessed that was part of what made her the Queen. She protected them to the best of her ability and the guardians lived to reciprocate.

The Queen drummed her fingers on the desk for a moment before bringing her eyes back to Keppin and then to Andy. She stood.

"Keppin, why don't you head back to class. I have something personal to discuss with Andy."

Andy could feel Keppin's disappointment at being dismissed but Keppin didn't show it to the Queen. He fist bumped Andy and left the room. The Director closed the door and leaned against it. With a long sigh, the Queen let her head sag forward, eyes closed before raising it again, a spark flashing in her gaze.

"I had wanted to explain your family history in such a way as to ease you into it. I had wanted to bring you to the lake where your parents were lost," she lamented. "But I have a situation I need your help with and because no outcome can really be predicted, I want to tell you now. Before I send you on your first true mission."

Andy's eyes went wide and his heart thumped. Two things he wanted more than anything in the world were being set at his feet.

The Queen's mouth pulled up slightly. "Not so fast, Andy. I wish it weren't so, but your family history does not exactly read the way of perfection." She winced at her own callous words but continued, "It's more like an odd soap opera."

Andy's mouth puckered like a fish. The Queen nodded at him.

"I had a sister," The Queen started. Her loss was palpable. Andy wanted to reach out and take her hand or kneel or something but instead he stayed still and listened.

"She married a lovely man, but it was a match of title, a family arrangement, not a love match." Andy blinked as he realized the Queen would have been brought up and lived through times when those things were important. It wasn't something most people concerned themselves with anymore. Andy couldn't imagine being told who he had to marry.

"They lived their lives, often separated but attending the right balls, visiting the correct contacts and then one day, Deirdre, my sister became with child."

Andy perked up. The Queen shook her head and continued.

"Your father, Thomas Chamberlain, who was a Baron no less, was her husband." Andy's jaw dropped. "Yes, he was a Guardian, but he was also a member of the peers, a gentleman first. And he needed an heir."

Andy sat back in his chair, head reeling from this information.

"My sister, Deirdre passed away during childbirth. The child, my niece, lived only a couple of days more."

"I am so sorry," Andy whispered.

"Deirdre was a tiny little thing. Weak from the start. How different we were. Her sweet nature could not beat out the condition of her body. She was many years older, but I still miss her. I suspect she's happier wherever she is now."

Andy nodded before something occurred to him. He frowned and looked at his hands, taking in their smooth caramel coffee coloring. The queen answered his silent question. "Your father's skin was as white as mine. There's so much more to this story."

Andy sat back, too stunned and intrigued to bother commenting. He could wait until she finished. Barely.

"Your mother..." the Queen began and then stopped. She was looking out the glass window of her office but clearly seeing something else.

"I never met your mother," she started again, "and I don't believe there are more than a handful of human people that have. If what your father said is true, she was what we call an Eelfae."

Andy's eyes widened. He had never heard of such a creature and yet its blood ran through his veins? How could he think of his mother that way?

She's not an *it.* Wait. He remembered his mother. She was no strange creature. He frowned and looked back at the Queen.

"Your father told me he met her in the Florida Keys. He said the bond was instant, there was no turning away. He'd been scuba diving at the time. After bonding, she followed him from the water. He taught her to speak English. He taught her to sail. It's kind of romantic when you think about the connection. They were happy."

She smiled while Andy fought to maintain his emotions. He looked at his hands again.

The Queen raised her chin in understanding. "Eelfae have a thick, black skin like a seal or a selkie. Before your father told me of her, I had thought them a myth or at least extinct. Turns out pheromones get the best of everyone once in a while. Thomas said she was tall, regal, delicate. And Powerful. They lived in the Keys happily and off the grid for almost two years."

The Queen paused to take a sip of tea. Andy blinked and did the same. She didn't wait for him to speak, just trudged forward with her story. *His* story.

"One day, not long after you were born, they were sailing. One minute she was happy and then her face fell as she stopped and seemed to listen intently to the wind. Thomas said she started to cry and couldn't stop. She held you and wept. Thomas didn't say for how long and he couldn't get her to explain. Finally, she put you down, kissed your forward and turned to him."

The Queen had tears gathering in her eyes and

she stopped to grab a tissue and dab them away before continuing.

"She told your father that he and you were the best thing she had ever done and hugged him fiercely. She said she was sorry, duty had called, and it was time for her to go. She told him to live a beautiful life and not to wait for her. Thomas said she changed into the most beautiful creature he'd ever seen before diving in and vanishing into the depths of the ocean."

The Queen paused to dab at her eyes. "He never would tell me what she looked like then. He waited for days and when the food was gone, he left only to came back again and again for months. You were so young, it was easy for him to entertain you on the boat. But she never came back. Several months later their bond broke. It had been but a thin line but still breathed with life until it snapped away. He was devastated. I almost lost him."

Andy couldn't stop the tears. Even though he knew she was not the mother from his memories, he mourned her loss, for himself and for his father. The Queen gave him a handful of tissues and sipped her tea patiently while he released his sadness. He wiped away the last of his loss and frowned.

"But I remember my mother," he said. The Queen nodded.

"Your father married again. It was not in him to keep you without a mother despite his lack of interest. Again, you must recall he was brought up in the world of the regal, the titled. He hired a competent nanny for you and continued along without marriage in mind. When he saw how well you did with Karen in your life, he married her and made you a complete family once more. You were four years old. She adored you and she completed you both. Thomas began to love her madly as the years passed. I hope your memories show you that he did indeed bond once more. He was very lucky to have found a bonded love twice in his lifetime."

A long sigh filled the room as Andy decompressed and blinked away the tears that threatened to erupt again. He gazed out the window to the sky.

"Feel like getting some air?" she asked. He stood abruptly and nodded. She gestured at the dressing screen. He rushed in, shed his clothes quickly and shifted. When he came out, the patio door was open, and he ran out and leapt into the air.

FOUND

Chapter 7

For weeks now small groups of Guardians had been scouring all the areas on the planet that were difficult for the Queen to access with her special links to the Guardians. The Queen had full confidence the Princess was being held in one of these areas.

The warehouse was so well hidden Connor might have missed it without the extra help. It had been Guardian Tio's intelligent foresight to bring a dragon with such far reaching senses along. Ollipeist, who lived secretly in one of the largest loughs in Ireland had been eager to get out for a bit. He kept on invisibility since the local lore had it that he had fled the country in times past. He had fled, true, but there was no where on Earth as lovely as his home of Ireland. The dragon had snuck back in and in exchange for the Guardians support, he returned the favor on occasion.

It was the scent of gun oil wafting uncharacteristically through the clear Irish air that finally led them to the warehouse. It was buried beneath the remains of an old tower home, now just crumbles of stone walls, rich green grass and ancient rocks. It was like any other hill and could have been found in so many places in

Ireland. The perfect place. Being near the water and on so much land, it was no wonder it had stayed hidden and they had gotten away undetected for so long.

Ollipeist had rooted around the ruins and it hadn't taken him long to find the entrance. Tio broke off the thick lock with a shifted claw and creaked open the double doors. A small dirt room was before them, with two open doorways on either side of the room. A salty draft ran through the room which led Connor to suspect these caves ran directly to the sea a half mile away.

If he was right, the cave fronts would exit at various places in the cliff side and any flying creature could come and go as they please, especially during the night.

Like a gargoyle. The thought sent shivers up Connor's spine. Next to a dragon, a gargoyle would be the perfect creature to bring goods to and from the mouth of high caves. A boat idling in the water below would be able to easily take or bring stock and none would be the wiser.

Another shiver and Connor turned to Tio. "You can be sure they know we're here," he commented.

"I'll call it in," Tio said. Connor nodded and Tio proceeded to pull his phone from his jeans pocket.

Seeing they had found that for which were searching, Ollipeist took to the sky at top speed, whooping in glee at his freedom. Since they couldn't see him, they only knew he was gone by the lack of his spirit in their vicinity.

While Tio waited for his call to connect,

FOUND

Connor edged forward, a dagger in each hand, to peer through the left doorway. He paused when he heard a familiar sound, a beast of legend. It was a sound he did not expect nor wish to hear at that very moment. He turned around while at the same time his skin began to swirl with the change. The Rak came through the right doorway.

RAAAK.

Tio dropped his phone and pulled out his sword. He ran over to stand beside Connor.

"I didn't think Rak's were in Europe," he stated as he took a stand.

"I'd heard rumors but never seen one before," Connor said as his shirt tore off his expanding and rippling body. He growled. The Rak raised a dark gray sword and swung toward him. Connor countered the heavy blow with one of his own. His dagger was not the equipment needed for this fight. Despite the Rak's human size, with its sinewy muscle it was fast and agile.

More noise erupted from the entrance on the other side of the room.

"There's too many," Tio hollered as his sword slammed into a fourth Rak. Connor had no time to answer. They were losing and he knew it.

"Been a pleasure, Tio!" he hollered even as a Rak sliced into his midsection. The sword was made of a substance that could penetrate even a Guardian's fool proof natural armor.

Tio wanted to tell Connor the same, but had no time to think of it further before the lights went out forever.

~~*~~

In the middle of the office, Helen Barrows fell to her knees, one hand clutching her heart and the other bracing her fall to the ground. Her face was scrunched in pain as large tears bled from her eyes and rolled heavily down her cheeks. The Director dropped down next to her and pulled her into his arms. Chest heaving with loss, she took comfort in his arms for a moment before straightening herself out. She sat, holding his hand and looked around the silenced room, meeting the eyes of everyone there while she shook her head.

"The Irish crew didn't make it."

She heard someone whimper, Jenny the analyst she thought, as she took to her feet.

"But I know where they are now," she snarled and walked to the map. She placed a finger on the spot, and someone lit it with red. The Guardian Queen pulled her finger away and turned to the Director.

"It's time to end this," she said through clenched teeth.

The Director nodded and turned to the room. "You heard her. I want a want a full work up of the area. I want it," he paused and looked at the clock on his phone, "in 30 minutes."

He looked at his wife. "You should take a breather," he told her softly so only she would hear. She reached over and squeezed his shoulder before walking to her office and sliding behind a privacy screen, stripping her clothes as soon as she was hidden.

She heard someone slide open the patio doors

and as soon as her clothes were off, she shifted. Stretching her second skin, she walked out the patio and gazed at the sunny sky. Pausing only to push back the rush of loss, she leapt off the patio and into the wind. Her wings beat to the rhythm of the earth's breath as she flew higher and higher.

The animals that could hear from such a distance froze when they heard the roar of the Queen howling her pain to the sky.

Chapter 8

Having a vague recollection of what the sky looked like in person, and a few picture books to hand, Lauren drew herself an ocean with a sunlit sky and a boat that would come and carry her away.

A shadow took away her lamp light and she glanced up.

"Oh hello, Marten," she said before scratching a curled line into the sky to represent a bird, just another thing she had not seen in so long she'd forgotten their true form.

"El," the gravelly voice said, "it's time."

Lauren blew out a frustrated sigh before putting down the colored pencil and standing. She no longer bothered to fight the inevitable. She followed the hulking man into the office where the doctor sat preparing the things he needed to draw her blood. She sat in the chair next to him and held out her arm.

"Hi, Doc." She let her head fall back gently and rest on the wall.

"Good morning, Lauren. How are you today?"

"Fine until now." She lowered her chin to glare at Marten. The Doctor made a sympathetic tsk before tying the rubber around her arm. He poked at her arm to locate a satisfactory vein before inserting the needle. Lauren sighed and closed her eyes. Once a week the doctor came and once a week, he took several tubes of her blood.

Next stop was the Witch's room. Lauren was scared of the Witch like no one else in this strange prison of hers. The woman was being controlled by Marten, that much was clear. How he was doing it was a mystery. The amount of power it must take to hide this prison from anyone on the outside was be spectacular, and that is exactly what the witch was doing. If only Lauren could figure out *why*.

Lauren thought anyone would be stupid not to be afraid of that kind of power. There had been a time when Lauren thought she could escape. Now she just watched and waited.

The Witch was weak today, Lauren observed when they entered the room. Her head drooped and long blond hair hung limply down past scrawny shoulders. Her arms were slack, the chains in the ceiling holding her upright. Another chain held a foot to the ground to constrict motion. Between the neglect of this woman and the blood loss, Lauren felt sick. She held a hand over her mouth to recover for a moment. Even a scary witch shouldn't be treated so poorly. Lauren's heart went out to her. She turned to Marten.

"When did you last give her a meal?"

He blinked and looked thoughtfully at the Witch before shrugging.

Lauren clenched her fists and rolled her eyes

to the ceiling. She wanted out, wanted away from this place but even she couldn't stay quiet and let another person die if she could help it.

"You're not going to get any worthy magic out of a dying Witch."

Marten raised his brows at her before leaving the room. A chair sat in the center of the room in front of a pedestal with a clean bowl resting on top. The Witch was hung on the other side. As soon as Lauren sat in the chair, the Witch's gold eyes opened and met hers. Fear streaked down Lauren's spine, but she couldn't look away.

The Witch's head pulled back slightly before she blinked and then closed her eyes once more. The Witch opened her mouth to speak but only a harsh breath came out. Lauren glanced around the room for water but there was nothing.

"Come."

Lauren heard the whisper and turned back to the Witch, whose eyes were still closed. She stood and moved to the pedestal, not allowing herself to get any closer. A zing of apprehension simmered in her veins and the loss of blood only added to her tangled thoughts.

The yellow eyes met hers one more.

"You're a leader," the dusty voice said, "your time comes soon. And I will be free once more."

Chills whispered through Lauren's skin. She watched as a droplet of blood formed on the Witch's cracked lips. A pale tongue whisked the blood away before it could gain any traction. Lauren fell back to the chair.

"Okay," she acknowledged. Her voice sounded

wimpy even to her own ears.

Marten chose that moment to walk in. He handled a bowl of broth to Lauren.

"I'll be back in fifteen minutes," he said before turning around and leaving the room again.

Lauren let out a breath before moving to feed the very creature casting the spells and hiding her from the rest of world.

Chapter 9

Verity wasn't sure the correct way to greet the Queen of the Fae, so she dipped into a deep curtsy, almost touching her nose to her knee before righting herself and looking at the Queen's neck.

The last time they had met, Verity had just freed Rothald from his kidnapper and had no idea what was in store for her.

"Well met, Verity Applebee. It has been some time since I have laid these eyes on your face."

Keeping her face from showing any confusion by the Queen's lilting speech, Verity dipped her head again.

"Thank you, Queen. It's nice to see you too."

"My son is pleased to have you visit his realm. In just a few hundred of your years he will take over and perhaps have time to see more of you."

Verity didn't think it would be wise to correct the Queen on her life expectancy.

"Sounds nice," she replied instead.

The Queen leaned in and put her hand on Verity's shoulder. A jolt of power punched through and Verity's knees buckled. Rothald grabbed her arm so she wouldn't topple over. When she had her footing once again, she could feel the steady hum of power in her veins.

"Well, isn't that interesting," the Queen said and released her shoulder. The power feed stopped and left Verity to feel an unexpected emptiness. The Queen continued speaking.

"Since you have found your way home, would you care to have the Changeling curse removed?"

Verity forgot herself and brought her head up abruptly to meet the Queen's eyes. They were the blue of a Kashmir sapphire. Rothald's were a mirror copy. The Queen's lips quirked to one side.

"You didn't know?" she commented. She had white hair that flowed down her back and halfway was captured in a long braid. Verity didn't immediately turn to dust or start croaking like a frog, so she doubted the truth to the rumors she'd heard about looking upon the Fae Queen.

Shaking her head, Verity affirmed, "I don't even know what you're talking about."

"What it is?" Duran asked as he entered Verity's space closer than she would have liked.

Rothald chuckled. "I was wondering," he said. "Something didn't appear right when I looked at her."

The Queen gestured toward Rothald who came to stand next to her. She pointed in Verity's direction, more above her than at her.

"Do you see the milky mist around her," she asked her son. He moved his head slightly to the left. Verity watched his pupils move strangely but so quickly she couldn't really understand what she saw.

"Ah."

Duran cursed.

"You see it brother?" Rothald queried.

"Yes," Duran groused. Verity frowned but before she could interrupt their lesson, the Queen spoke again.

"Now this one is unusual because it has a spell attached to it. One created by someone powerful and knowledgeable enough to conceal the mist from most of us."

"But who cou..." Verity was cut off by Duran.

"I didn't even think to look at her differently."

The Queen gazed at her oldest son, not with complete animosity but a loathing Verity was certain Duran probably deserved.

"Mediocre, my *son*. Just like your father," she said before asking. "A small oversight, don't you think?"

Duran didn't answer, just took a step away from the small group. Verity studied him for a moment as he stared daggers at his mother. She observed his dark hair and lavender eyes, a stark contrast to his mother. Rothald was obviously his mother's son in looks at least, both being on the light side. It was a curious observation Verity would ask Duran about one day, if she felt adventurous.

"How do you see the spell?" Rothald wanted to know. Verity determined she was akin to a science experiment at that moment.

"You don't see it with your eyes. Since you did not see the mist, you know there is a spell in place. This is something rare indeed." She met Verity's eyes once more. A shiver ran down Verity's back, but it wasn't painful or surprising. It felt odd, like an awareness settling in, she just didn't know what yet.

"Do you wish to have it removed, child?"

"What is *it*?" Verity finally got her words in. "And why is it hidden?"

The Queen sniffed and then turned to sit on her throne. She waved a hand, and someone brought a chair over for Verity. Duran took a seat to the Queen's left and Rothald to her right. They stared at her in silence. The Queen inspected her long fingernails before accepting a flute of something bright orange and bubbling.

She brought it to her lips and spat in it. Verity couldn't help the yelp of surprise.

Rothald chuckled and Duran glared.

"You are a Changeling," the Queen declared.

"But..." Verity started but the Queen's eyebrows raised, and she held out a hand.

"Patience. A Changeling infant is one who has been left with a human family in exchange for their human child."

Silence fell as Verity looked at each of them expectantly. Then it dawned on her. They were saying that her parents were not her own. They were saying she was Fae. Full, one hundred percent Fae heritage. Verity sat back in her chair. The adrenaline in her system was out of control.

The idea of it was preposterous. Being a healer, wouldn't she have noticed her own inadequacies as a human?

Understanding sunk even further. She was a healer. It wasn't even that part of her human side was a healer or maybe her spiritual side was the healer. It was the Fae blood that ran through her. Verity barely contained her sob.

"Ah, yes," the Queen whispered, "there she sees now."

She sat up and held the flute out to Verity. "Drink this and all will be revealed."

Still reeling from the revelation, Verity grimaced with the memory of the Queen spitting in the drink.

"Take it," Duran demanded. Verity frowned at him.

"What will happen to me?" Verity asked.

"Your true self will be revealed," the Queen said with a shrug. It seemed strange and practiced. "You will have to learn to glamour yourself as you will never look human again without it."

Verity pressed her lips together. Freeing herself from the curse would likely bring about untold changes and compilations. What if she was a troll or a pixie? How much of her life would she be able to get back?

The one thing she did believe was the truth was stronger and better than having oneself hidden by magic. She took the flute.

"Bottom's up," she murmured and tipped it into her mouth.

The pain lasted only moments. It was like burning your arm on the inside of the oven or the side of a sizzling pan, only it zapped her entire body.

FOUND

There was a loud pop and her senses opened all at once. Sounds were piercingly loud before settling down into a dull roar. The scent in the air became cloying and she could feel the grain in the wood of the chair she sat upon. She kept her eyes clamped shut for fear of what she would see. The explosion of color behind her lids was overwhelming. She could feel the nerves and noises and motions of the insides of her skin. Everything was sensitive and it was difficult to discern individual things without concentration.

"Well, isn't this surprising," the Queen commented. Verity held her hands over her eyes as she sat partially curled in the chair.

"Why, she's quite lovely, mother." Rothald's awed voice filtered through.

"Indeed," the Queen said. Verity heard a grunt from Duran.

"My children, it is apparent you had a relative hidden away in the human realm."

Shock forced Verity's startled eyes open. She closed them again, the world being too vivid at first glance. She slowly blinked and gradually was able to tolerate her strangely bright vision.

"You will become used to it." The Queen's hand patted her on the head.

"Welcome to the family," Rothald confirmed. Duran spat some human curse words and walked away. Rothald took Verity's arm.

"I think maybe some time alone to adjust would be helpful," Rothald consoled as she stood on shaky legs and leaned into him. "I will escort you to a room and have food brought to you. We will talk tomorrow."

Verity was too shocked and too drained to protest. He brought her to a stunning green and blue room with a huge canopy bed. He bowed at the door before leaving her alone. The room seemed to dampen the noise around her. Verity kicked off her shoes and crawled into the bed. Sleep pervaded her body and she sank into darkness.

Chapter 10

"There! She's back there!" Sloane shouted while pointing toward the back of the quaint little house. Liam ran along its side with Sloane at his heels. He didn't wait for an invitation. He pulled the shed's door off its hinges and tossed it to the ground. It was empty except for a row of neatly hung gardening tools, a tall ladder and an extra-large plastic chest.

A sob escaped Sloane's throat when she saw the chest. Liam strode over and with a fist, broke the thick lock. Sloane grappled with the metal and dropped it to the floor. Liam lifted the lid and the old scents of dirty bodies, rotting food and stale water wafted up. Sloane sensed only one inhabitant. The heat outside was unbearable without also being locked away. Sloane couldn't imagine being practically buried.

Peering down, Sloane barely contained another sob. All she saw was blackness below. The bottom of the chest had been cut away and had covered a small underground chamber.

"It's okay!" she hollered as sweetly as possible. "We're here to rescue you!"

A whimper followed by a sniffle rose from the depths. Liam prepared to jump. Sloane held up a hand.

"We're going to get you out of there! I need you to get as close to a wall as you can so my Knight in Shining Armor can get down there, okay?"

A shuffling noise was followed by another whimper and a high pitched noise.

Sloane nodded at Liam who jumped.

A startled cry was followed by a whoosh of air and then Liam was standing next to Sloane once more holding a small, dirty girl with tear streaks down her face. Sloane moved to take the child, who she guessed was about six years old, and cradled her gently. She backed out of the shed into the sunshine and waited while Liam took pictures of the shed, the chest and then back down in the hole.

The child shook in her arms.

"It's going to be okay, now," Sloane said as she rubbed circles on the girl's back.

"How did you find her?" someone asked in a pleasant, older female voice. Just like Grandma. Sloane froze. The girl started to cry uncontrollably. Something bony pushed into Sloane's back.

"Now you both can get down there. There you go," the voice said as a gnarled hand nudged her back toward the shed.

"I don't think so, shrew." Liam's voice was steel.

"Oh, another. I'm going to have so much fun!" Whatever was behind Sloane chuckled.

"I'm afraid not," Liam countered. There was a

rush of wind and then whatever was standing behind her, grew in enough proportions to block out the sun. Sloane rushed toward the shed, and then veered to its left and turned to peer around the side.

The owner of the voice had broken from its glamor and was now at least three feet taller than Sloane's substantial height of almost six feet. Liam stood in front of the bluish green troll in his human form.

Sloane didn't wait to see what happened. She knew Liam would be okay. She turned away and ran toward the front of the house with the child clinging to her. Her car was at the end of the street where Liam had left it and she headed in that direction. A roar thundered behind her and Sloane sincerely hoped Liam shut it up before the neighborhood decided to investigate.

A second roar boomed around them, and Sloane rolled her eyes. Liam. A moment before she reached the car, another came around the corner and stopped next to her. The window was down, and Kam's scarred, anxious face stared out. Sloane pointed down the street.

"Fifth house down on the right, back yard."

The car zipped away. She wouldn't need to call anyone for help now, not like Liam needed it. Sloane opened the back door of her car before looking into the girl's face. "I'm going to put you down in the back seat here. There's some fruit and water for you. Have some of that while I turn the car on so we can cool down, all right?"

The girl nodded timidly, and Sloane put her

down before closing the door gently. As she went around the car, she texted her Uncle Henry. He would meet them at the house and bring toys and movies. He always helped to care for the children she collected from the nightmares. Sloane shuddered and pushed away her own memories before turning on the car and slipping into the other side of back seat to wait for Liam. She had to smile when she saw her little friend Bob, a Brownie with a heart of gold who showed up in the form of a squirrel. He couldn't help it and comforted her rescues when he was able. Bob winked at her before curling into the side of the now smiling little girl.

FOUND

Chapter 11

Andy came back to the Queen's office a couple of hours later. He shifted to human and the Queen shooed him off to get a meal before they sat together again in her office, this time with hot chocolate.

"Delicious," Andy said after his first sip. "My family history is surreal." She smiled.

"I'm glad you think of it that way. I know your father would be happy to know that."

"What happened to him and Karen?" he asked.

The Queen pressed her lips together. "You all went out for dinner one night. You were eight I believe. They were driving over a bridge and it collapsed. We don't believe it was an accident but," she shrugged, "we were never able to get enough evidence to show otherwise to the humans. I know of many a creature who could cause that kind of havoc and easily be mistaken for a dynamite explosion or something similar. There was not much we could do."

Andy's shoulders slumped and he looked at the floor without seeing. He tried to recall the accident and being in the water. Anything. The only thing he knew for certain was that, with the exception of a shower, he did not like water and had never learned to swim, staying away from anything having to do with it. He would have laughed at the irony if he didn't miss them so much.

The Queen leaned forward in her chair, bringing her hands together in her lap as she looked at Andy. "The most interesting part of the story, Andy, is the fact you were found sitting on the beach, dry and calm. The only evidence you had been in the car was the torn seatbelt still hanging off your shoulder and a bit of seaweed in your hair."

Andy sat upright. "What?"

"My sentiments exactly. When was the last time you went swimming, Andy?"

"I don't," he insisted with a wave of his hand like he was batting away a fly. The Queen acknowledged him with a grunt and stood.

"All right, if you have any questions for me, let me know. I will do my best to answer them. But I do have some pressing matters to cover with you. I am sorry to push you after giving you this story, but it is quite important. It affects the entire den and I need your help."

Andy blew out a breath that did little to calm him and nodded enthusiastically. "I think that would be a good distraction," he said. "What can I do?"

"I need your help to find someone. You and a team, Sloan and Liam included. Your Displacer skills will be an asset."

"Who are we looking for?"

"My protege. Your future Queen."

Chapter 12

Verity woke and sat up quickly, turning her body to sit on the side of the bed while she acclimated to the room. It was dim, though she could sense the sun and see light trickling through the edges of a curtain hanging in the single window. Waking up had never been so easy. She didn't even feel like she needed a coffee or tea to become coherent.

But she felt weird. She was herself no question. Her thoughts were still her own, or at least it seemed so.

Her body however was a different story. Her senses overwhelmed her. It was difficult to cope. Until this moment she only believed in the standard five senses but now she knew better. There were so many more. She was betting everyone had them but didn't notice since it was just always there.

She knew where the sun was located, and the moon. She knew at how many beats per minute her heart raced. She could feel the blood pumping through her veins. Veins that stretched throughout her body and she felt every one of them. There was so much more to inspect but she would hold off on the exploration.

She usually had on sparkly lipstick and thick black eyeliner. Her light auburn hair was usually dyed black. The wavy hair that flowed down her shoulder and reached her elbows was a vibrant red.

She needed a mirror.

She stood and found her legs strong, and her movements smooth. Surveying the room, she found the mirror quickly. They were surprisingly the doors to the closet. The Fae were so human and so not. Shock stole her breath when she looked into the glass.

She hadn't changed in height, but everything else was more defined. The mirror confirmed the fire engine red hair. There wasn't a trace of black dye to be found. Her eyes were usually a subtle green. Now they were reminiscent of sparkling emeralds. Verity guessed they would end up being lighter or darker depending on her moods, as she had noticed with Duran.

Duran, she abruptly realized, was now a very close relative. She scowled in distaste. So weird.

Then she noticed the pale ears that subtly protruded from the mass of red hair. She quickly moved her hair out of the way and inspected ears that elongated into an elegant tip. She explored it briefly with her fingertips before dropping the hair and staring wide eyed at the stranger in the mirror.

Herself, her spiritual self, check. The rest of her. Nope and nope. Verity wondered if she would ever feel normal again.

FOUND

Verity took a hot shower and found a flowing blue dress in the wardrobe before opening the door to the outside to discover what was next in this adventure.

Duran was leaning against a low wall covered in vines. Birds sang in a nearby bush. The air was warm but sweet. Verity breathed in deep before meeting Duran's eyes. His lips were quirked up.

"Greetings, *cousin*." He smirked. Verity rolled her eyes before noticing Duran's eyes were vibrant and clashed against his dark locks. There was just something different about this place. She must have been staring too long. Duran stepped up to her, only inches away.

"It's because you're in your *proper* place," he affirmed as though he'd read her mind.

"What is your problem?" Verity wondered.

"You were supposed to be the answer," he sneered. Something about him revolted her. Without thinking Verify shoved him. He flew back, crashing against the low wall and flipping over it, and vanishing behind.

"Oh!" Verity shrieked, "Duran!" She ran over to the wall and looked over. Duran lay in a bed of black and white flowers laughing. He bent forward and stood with a single jump before hopping over the wall to stand next to her.

"You might still be of some use with that kind of power," he commented.

Verity's eyes widened before her blood started sizzling beneath her skin. She shoved a finger on his chest.

"What makes you think I would want to help

you with anything? You have done nothing but make me feel like an unwanted outcast despite the fact that apparently I'm your relation!"

Duran stepped back and looked at his chest. The spot where Verity's finger had been was smoking. His lip quirked. "Ow," he said before blowing softly on his chest. Verity's hand went to her mouth.

"Oh my god," she whispered.

"Brother! I see you met well with our cousin this morning." Rothald's voice was clear and close behind Verity's shoulder. She turned and the hard glint in his eyes showed Verity for the first time that Rothard was more aware than she had thought.

"Good morning, Rothard," she greeted him with a smile.

"Cousin," he said and held out an arm. "Come break your fast with me."

"Of course," Verity agreed and took his arm. As they strode out of the small cove, Verity glanced behind her and met Duran's inquisitive eyes before his mouth quirked and she turned forward again.

"You will need to learn to control your magic before you can leave," Rothald commented as their leisurely walk brought them toward a small meadow. There were scattered tables covered in light fabrics and serving plates filled with various foods. Some were foreign and exotic to Verity and others were the simple breakfast foods Verity had grown up with.

Her heart missed a beat then. She missed home.

There were young Fae boys and girls holding trays with colored pitchers and clear goblets. Verity panicked when she remembered being told never to eat food or drink supplied by the Fae. Then she remembered that she was one. And being with Rothald surely she would have some protection. She hoped.

A small boy came up to her elbow and held out one of the clear goblets. She took it and the boy waited patiently as he held up a tall purple-gold pitcher and short squat yellow pitcher.

"He's offering you wine." Rothald gestured at the purple container. "Or honey mead."

"Uh," Verity said and frowned. "Do you have any water?"

The boy frowned at her for just a moment before reaching a fist into the air. When he opened his fist slightly, water trickled from it. Verity stared it while Rothald took her mug-holding hand and pushed it toward the water. She held it under the trickle and the boy opened his fist a bit further to increase the flow. When the mug was almost full, the boy closed his fist, pushed into the air and then walked away.

Verity took a sip. The water was cool and fresh as though it had run through layers of granite to arrive. She hummed with satisfaction. Rothald laughed.

"Soon you'll be able to do that yourself," he declared, "at least here."

They found a table and Verity ate heartily, never seeming to fill up but feeling satisfied. She could get used to that.

"What's next?" she asked Rothald as they stood.

"I must get to work but for you, I have a surprise."

Verity tensed. A surprise from a Fae, even from one as sweet as Rothald, was likely not one she would be excited about.

He took her arm and as they walked, the scenery slowly changed from green meadows and black and white flowers to a stone cobbled road with quaint cottages stacked one next to the other. Decorated signs announced the vocation of the inhabitants. Parsel's Apothecary, Winchell's Chimes and Charms, Froggy Toes and More. Verity's face scrunched in distaste and she stopped reading the placards until they stopped in front of one.

School of Ivy.

Verity turned to a smiling Rothard. "You'll have fun," he reassured her as he opened the door.

A small foyer led to a large room that was currently occupied by a circle of Fae. They were children. Inside the circle and sitting back to back were two grown Fae ladies. One of them had hair of Ivy. Verity presumed she was the headmistress and owner of the school.

As they moved into the room, the two adults turned to the door. With the exception of the hair, they were identical. The other had long straight locks of dark chestnut. Neither blinked as they looked at her before rising and bowing to Rothald. He bowed back.

"My friends," he stated, "please meet Verity. She saved my life when I was a child and has just discovered her Fae heritage. I implore you to teach her our ways as best you can. She was raised on the Earth realm."

Some of the children Fae gasped and others whispered excitedly.

Rothald left with a bow and Verity stood, uncomfortable in her own skin and embarrassed to be deposited in what she considered grade school. The teachers attempted civility by standing and motioning for Verity to sit with the group. Looking over the children, Verity met eyes full of awe, contempt and puzzlement. No one moved as they sat in their perfect circle and watched her.

"I don't bite," Verity announced.

Several of the children smiled and one girl moved over a few inches in an effort to make room for Verity. A boy in his teens she guessed, next to her got up, glaring and went to lean against the wall. As Verity walked past him to sit in his spot, she offered a solemn thank you. The only way she knew he'd heard was by the slight nod. Verity guessed he was only being nice because the Prince himself had dropped her off.

As Verity sat down, the girl who had made room for her smiled ever so briefly flashing sharp teeth. Verity raised a brow and the girl whispered, "I bite," before bringing her eyes back to the teachers. Verity swallowed.

When the lesson ended Verity was speechless. The class was about finding your magic. Though she had not realized it at the time, Verity already knew how to find her magic. It was part of what fueled her ability to heal. During class, when she had first reached out for the power she knew was there, the change was only too obvious. Bigger, stronger. More.

She sat on a bench outside Winchell's Chimes and Charms and held her hands out. The glare of sun on the sand seemed to make them glow. She made fists and then stretched them out again.

A shadow fell over her hands, the gold glow becoming a gray pallor. She placed them on her knees and brought her head up to meet Duran's violet eyes. They froze as they looked at each other for a moment before Verity nodded.

"I will try, Duran. I can only imagine what you are going through, and I will try. Just give me a few days to find my," she lifted her hands and looked them over again, "my understanding."

"I will explain more tomorrow, it might help," he replied. He turned and took one step before vanishing like smoke.

Verity blinked before standing herself. She wasn't quite sure what to do with herself.

She felt one someone walk up and stand next to her.

"He suffers," the female said.

Verity sighed. "I see that now."

"Your power has a strong sound."

Verity looked up and found it was the teacher with long strands of Ivy hair. She wanted to touch it and see what it felt like. She'd barely had the thought when several strands reached toward her. Verity jumped back and the teacher laughed.

"I'm afraid it does sometimes have a mind of its own. They call me Ivy," she said and gave Verity a small nod. Verity gave a meek smile and sighed softly.

"Just when I thought I was getting used to things, something happens to disabuse me of the idea. I have quite a bit to learn."

"The learning never ends, child. It is a thing of forever like the magic in all things, or death."

Verity frowned and nodded. She wasn't sure what to say.

Ivy pointed down the road. "If you follow this road for some time, you will come to a body of water. Look for the sun statue, then turn north. You will end up at the home of your kin. Be sure not to step off the path. There are many things that make the land their home and would not appreciate you stomping around it."

"Thank you very much," Verity said, feeling awkward and self-conscious around this woman. "I'll see you tomorrow then."

"Yes," the woman replied and then vanished in a similar puff to Duran.

Verity wondered if she would ever learn to do that as she headed down the street. The one thing that had been bothering her was her kin. Her *family*. They kept saying she was family, but nobody had bothered to explain *how*. Or possibly more important, *who*.

FOUND

Chapter 13

Dealing with trolls was annoying. They didn't die easily or quietly and if there was one thing Liam needed right now, it was a nice, quiet death. The troll had managed to get itself settled into the perfect family neighborhood. It was only missing a white picket fence.

The troll in front of him wasn't the biggest he'd seen or beaten, but it wasn't small either. Without being able to shape shift, he was about to get quite the workout. The creature was lucky the little girl was still whole, or he'd be in a much worse mood. Just thinking of the hole where the child had been kept brought a fiery heat to Liam's chest.

The troll beat its chest and then lunged. Since it wasn't feasible for him to change in a public area, Liam had to beat this thing in his weaker form. He dodged the creature. Trolls were smart but not skilled fighters, generally demonstrating a lumbering, whack-a-mole method. This one stumbled but quickly swung around again. A huge fist shot out faster than Liam expected. He felt the breeze of the motion on his cheek as he dipped and swung back up to lob a fist into its left ear.

Growling, it stuck out an impressive foot

thinking to trip Liam, but he jumped over it and while in the air, shoved with both feet. They both hit the ground, and Liam was up again within a moment. The troll pushed itself up, a furious expression on its wrinkled face.

A shadow of a figure blended along the side of the house toward the back, unnoticed despite the brightness of the day. Reaching the backyard, it solidified and rammed into the back of the troll's legs. It fell with a solid thud and Liam wasted no time snapping it neck and then stomping with extra force on its back, breaking the spine.

He reached out a hand to pull Kam up.

"Glad you could show up." He grinned at his friend and fellow Guardian.

"Well, I was going to go grocery shopping with Jaws, but this seemed more important." Kam smiled, the long scar running up the side of his face making the teddy bear of a Guardian look like a deranged lunatic.

Liam chuckled as he grabbed one leg of the troll, and gestured at the other. Kam grabbed it and they pulled the troll toward the shed.

"How is Jaws?" Liam asked while watching the grass pop back up in the trail of the troll.

"She's great actually," Kam said, a dreamy smile on his otherwise scared face. "She's settling into human society surprisingly well and her sisters are loving the attention. Although having them all together while they learn the ropes is a huge pain in the ass."

Liam laughed as they reached the open chest. Kam dropped the troll leg and looked inside. He growled softly before turning and with a quick stomp, crushed the bones of the recently dropped foot. They pulled the body up and dropped it into the hole. Liam closed the lid and then picked up the recently discarded shed door and propped in into place.

"I'll let them know there's a cleanup in the happy family neighborhood," Kam said.

"Thanks, man. I need to get Sloane home to clean up the little girl and then we have to contact the authority's and see if her parents are still around." Knowing the likelihood of that, Kam simply nodded.

"Sloane's really got a knack for finding lost ones," Kam commented when they got to his car.

"I know," Liam agreed. "I'm glad she only goes tracking a few times a month. Otherwise, I may have to open my own childcare. The bastards are really busy during the summer."

"So much for some time off to get to know your bride better," Kam teased as he slid into his seat.

"Oh, don't you worry, Kam. I'm getting to know her just fine."

Kam snickered before driving away. Liam made his way to the car where his wife and a scared little girl were cooling down in the air conditioning. He hoped the girl would be lucky enough to have some semblance of a normal life again. He always hoped for them. Even after a run in with one of the things that go bump in the night.

Chapter 14

Lauren had a plan.

She drummed her hands on the desk before her as the teacher explained geography. Who actually cared about how many types of dirt there were in the world? Dirt surrounded Lauren and all she wanted was to get *out* of it.

If Lauren's figures were right, she had just passed her sixteenth birthday. She felt positive everyone in the prison had shifted to a higher level of alertness. Or watchfulness. Something, she felt, was different and yet the same Guardians from the day before were bled to feed the Witch's spell and the same cook was making her dinner and the same teacher was helping her with geography. The questions she had were endless.

After years of being in captivity, Lauren had developed some idea of what was going on. She overheard things. She crept around the building when Marten came to visit. He always had tidbits from the outside world. And guns. And bags of things that were whisked away from her reach. She had tried on several occasions to make her way through the dirt maze, toward the rich smell of sea salt but every time, someone caught her. The last time it had been Rawlins. He had promptly shot one of the Guardians and then hollered for a new one to be brought in. Even though he had not killed the man, it was enough. Lauren never tried to escape again.

That had been years ago. Without having attempted to escape again, Lauren was certain she had finally figured out enough clues, enough habits to truly find her way out. Now, since her one and only *talk* with the Witch, Lauren had been expecting something to happen.

When it had, she hadn't imagined it would be so painful.

Lauren lay in her bed sweating profusely. The pain was becoming a simmer in her veins. This was the third time today.

She had woken to the torment of a cat shredding her back, but found no evidence of any physical damage. Throughout the morning, she walked on delicate toes, leery of any ache or pain. Just as she finished lunch the pain struck again. She had raced to the restroom and curled on the floor clenching her teeth to avoid screaming. And now it had happened again as she prepared for bed.

She had no option but to wait for something magnificent to happen. It was the only way she could think of to get through the soul crushing horror of things moving under her skin. She felt from the bottom of her heart that whatever it was, she would find out very soon.

There was no doubt in her mind she could not tell anyone about what was happening, especially Marten. Sometime, hopefully very soon, things would change.

The questioning looks between the guards who kept her prisoner and the thoughtful looks from the ailing guardians were significant. They expected something, too. Lauren wondered if they suspected her. It felt like they were wondering and nothing more. Well, Lauren wasn't going to give anyone a hint.

She knew she was the one they wanted. She didn't know why or how, she just *knew*. She had no friends. She had no family, unless you counted Marten who said he was her Uncle, but no Uncle of Lauren's could be so horrid and so evil, blood or not, she would never grant him the title.

So, she planned. And she waited.

Chapter 15

Once the little girl was safely in the home of Sloane's uncle and playing quietly with another child, a little boy named Charles they had rescued last month, Sloane let herself slump in the passenger seat of the car while Liam drove them home.

He kept glancing over at her and it warmed her heart. Gone were the days where they frowned and bitched at each other. Really it had been more her bitching and him grunting in acknowledgment. Here were the days where she could be at peace with herself, the fact she was an Aspie and...she paused mid thought and smiled.

"What?" Liam asked with a gleam in his eye. Sloane chuckled and slapped his arm. He wiggled his eyebrows.

"You have a one track mind," she accused.

"Looking at you will do that to a man," he commented, quirking his mouth to the side.

"Whore," Sloane said with narrowed eyes. His smile broadened.

"Only with you, love. Now what were you smiling about?"

"I was recollecting the days when I thought I was cursed. Never to find love and never to have peace. You give me peace, among other things," she said as she reached over and gently squeezed his muscled thigh. "Among other things." Liam lifted his brows twice in succession before putting his eyes back on the road.

"And finding out about Aspies? Things could settle down for me then."

Sloane glanced out the window as the palm trees and strip malls flew by.

"I'm happier than I ever thought possible."

Liam didn't answer right away, and Sloane knew why. The softest breath left his full lips before he turned to her briefly. "You make me happy," he said.

Squeezing his thigh again before folding her hands together in her lap, Sloane answered, "But you're restless."

He nodded. "I am."

"I've told Helen as much."

"What?" Liam looked at her in surprise.

She smiled. "I can't worry about you forever and hold you back from the things that make you who you are." She blinked back the unexpected liquid pooling in her eyes. "I know you love the hunt, the chase, the capture of the bad things. I can't keep you from it and keep you happy. Our monthly outings aren't enough and I'm finally okay enough to let you go."

His head swung sharply and concerned eyes searched her face.

She shook her head quickly. "Not like that, you're not getting rid of me that easily."

He smiled. "You sure about this?"

FOUND

He pulled the car into their driveway and Sloane looked at the cute house with shrubs, a mailbox, and a cat skulking its way over from the side yard probably to cry about his current level of starvation.

"I'm sure," she said. "I have my online business, my friends, and my crafts to keep my busy. You need something too." She glanced at the neighbor's house, the one that was constantly stopping by to borrow tools or invite them to barbeques. "I know Steve doesn't fill all those boxes for you."

Liam laughed as they got out of the car.

Sloane met him at the walkway to the house and he pulled her to him, disregarding the blanket of heat in the air. She snuck her arms around him.

"Mine," he whispered. Sloane shrieked when he pulled her up and slung her over his shoulder.

"You are such a barbarian," she squealed as she gave his backside a squeeze.

"And you're a tart," he said as he let them into the house.

A couple of days later they got a call. Sloane was surprised to have herself included in the request. Within hours they were tucked in together on a plane to France.

They were off to see the Queen.

Chapter 16

The sun statue was not what Verity was expecting. She sorely wished she had sunglasses when she rounded a bend and came upon it. Ducking her head from the blazing light, she squeezed her eyes closed to try and allow them to adjust somehow. The light was painful and yet she felt no heat. Each time she tried to open her eyes even slightly, she found them closing tight again.

"Oh come on," she complained. It didn't help that buried not very far down, her gut was screaming for her to pay attention. This place was not safe for someone who did not know the lay of the land, and she clearly had no idea what was going on most of the time. The thought of hanging out with the Goblin's in the lair suddenly became a much more pleasant thought than it once was.

A faint whispering to her left sent chills up her back. Verity opened her eyes only to have them slam closed again. This was ridiculous. How did anyone get around here? She sent vile thoughts at Ivy for her lack of warning.

She tried to remember if she had turned away from her destination when she'd come across the sun statue or had veered off into a different direction. The whispering was urgent and Verity stopped to listen.

The lilting language was unfamiliar, but Verity somehow made out the meaning.

Follow the air.

She brought her head up, keeping her eyes squeezed tight and felt for a breeze. It was there, a soft flowing current tickling her neck and grazing her clothes.

Once again, Verity found herself stuck. Was the voice encouraging her in deception or was there actually a nice little gnome family or perhaps pixies running around helping clueless humans, rather newly discovered Fae, to get around the oddities of this world.

Having little choice, Verity followed the breeze. She found herself going forward for only a short time before turning slightly to the right which would be correct if she was veering North. She went on, continuing to test her vision until at last, after blinking for several moments, she could see once more.

The landscape had changed quite a bit but the smell in the air was familiar. Verity wondered when she had started to notice smells so keenly. She admired the dark blue flowers on a tree as she passed and could have sworn it reached toward her. She picked up her steps and came over a hill to be greeted by a dotting of little cottages, thick grass, and small creatures that roamed like sheep but looked more like furry elephants. All of which led up to a large structure that resembled a tree house that had been added to over many, many years by completely different builders. Verity blinked at the chaos of color that greeted her. Some sections were light blue, some were a dark forest green, others were yellow and yet another was orange. Verity hoped her particular family was not responsible for it.

There was only one way to find out. She moved to pass a stunning violet unicorn grazing on some type of giant clover. It made a startled whinny and then tore away kicking up grass in its wake. With a frown, Verity headed toward the monstrosity of a building.

When she was closer, she could see clearly that each part of the building had its own front door, similar to the set up on the lane where she had attended her magic lesson. A window opened in a faded blue section above her and Verity squinted to see what might be lurking there. Something shoved her to the ground, and she shrieked as her knees and elbow were skinned by the rough dirt. Once she realized a heavy nothingness was pinning her down, she attempted to scream. It had barely started to leave her mouth when something else heavy landed on top of her and yet it had actually landed on top of whatever was already lying on her. Her scream was lost as the air was pushed from her lungs.

The heavy nothingness rolled off her and she watched dust poof up from the ground where it landed and then float up a bit further away as a large metal pot rolled to a stop. Despite the throbbing in her knees, Verity could see that whatever had pushed her to the ground had also saved her from being squashed. She glanced up and the window that had been open earlier was now closed. She had no way of knowing whether the incident had been an accident.

Glancing at her knees Verity sighed before turning toward the invisible person that had saved her. She stopped and stared. It was not a person but a beast. It lay spread on the ground, the fluorescent green fur on its chest rose and fell but the eyes she knew would glow red were closed. A Vigilo.

Around the size of a large German Sheppard, she had been chewed on by one once and wasn't interested in repeating the experience.

Her heart thumped as she backed up slowly, trying to make as little noise as possible. She debated calling for Rothald and wondered if it would still work to get his attention.

The Vigilo whimpered and something tugged in her chest. She took another step back, her eyes never leaving the creature's face when her peripheral caught sight of a green liquid oozing from its shoulder.

Stopping she watched it for a moment.

Damn.

Glancing at the sky in disbelief, she walked over to the animal and slowly knelt at its side. The gash was deeper than she'd originally thought. She guessed the pot had hit it and cracked the bone while splitting the skin.

Verity put her hands on either side of the

wound and started gently pushing it together. The Vigilo whined and its back leg shook. The eyes stayed closed. She pushed her magic into the wound, willing the cut to mend. Verity almost pulled away as the skin moved incredibly fast beneath her fingers.

The Vigilo growled and lifted its head. The eyes opened to reveal the bright, glowing red Verity was all too familiar with. She jumped to her feet and started backing away slowly. The healing had been too fast she realized. It would have hurt pretty badly. The creature growled again before laying its head back down and closing its eyes.

Tears of relief and pain touched Verity's eyes. She dropped her head and moaned. Damn her need to fix broken things. She went back and without delay laid her hands back beside the cut and this time, opened her herself up to just a trickle of the power. She felt the energy churn in her blood, pump through her veins and settle in just below her skin as it waited to be used. Ever so subtly she pushed it into the Vigilo's shoulder, giving more and more until she saw the slow winding and blending of skin. The creature's physical make-up might be foreign to her, but her magic knew what to do.

This. This was what made Verity tick, and now, the energy she had to heal was tenfold. She would gladly die trying to help others with this gift.

The front paws of the Vigilo stretched. Despite its dog-like qualities, she noticed for the first time its paws were more like a cat with a larger pad and claws tucked away. It also had a fifth digit like a thumb. That was disturbing.

Red eyes opened and watched her as she let her magic slowly close the wound and rejoin the cells and bone. Fear crawled up her spine, through her neck and into her head. The red eyes blinked and looked away as a deep sigh left the creature. Verity decided she was safe for the moment. The anxiety settled into the background while she worked. She felt it when the healing was not done, but safe. She was at a point where the remaining healing could be done naturally without the creature making it worse.

She pulled away her fingers slowly. The Vigilo's big head lifted and red eyes watched her. The fear came back as terror and she froze. The Vigilo huffed and the warmth of its breath rushed across her cheeks. Cinnamon. The smell registered in the background of her mind. A black tongue shot out of its fanged mouth and swept across her cheek. Before she could react, its big body rolled up from the ground and vanished.

Verity didn't move as her eyes looked everywhere for evidence of the beast. Her ears strained for the slightest sound. She stood slowly, her heart trying to escape her chest. She heard a huff. Then a small whine. The air flickered a few feet to her right and her eyes hurt from staring. She saw a bending shimmer in the space and then the Vigilo came to view. It sat with its head held high and tongue lolling from its mouth. Thick drool dripped intermittently to the sandy dirt.

Once again, Verity backed up. She wondered

why no one else was around. She thought the village would be teaming with people, or Fae or whatever. Even the other animals seemed to have vanished. She glanced at the Vigilo again. He still sat quietly and watched her. She felt a little like it was laughing at her.

Since it wasn't attacking, Verity stopped trying to figure it out and turned away, heading around the weird tree house to see if her new Fae family was on the other side. She glanced behind her once and found the beast had vanished again. She wondered just how long it had been following her.

Finally! It seemed like Verity had been walking for hours but she guessed it was because her mind was racing with thoughts of having her guts gouged out or dying of hunger. The familiar field where she had dined before appeared over the second hill past the weird tree house building and a little to the left. The light purple grass was a welcome relief. No one would likely attack her now. With that thought, a bustle of activity exploded onto the field and small groups of Fae walked out of the air and into the space. Verity followed, glancing around and hopeful for a familiar face.

As she stepped foot onto the field, a small boy with pointed ears joined her. He held out a cup and Verity took it gladly. Taking a sip, the honeyed water was both refreshing and rejuvenating. She felt the extra strength in her step and headed directly to the tables.

As she looked over the plethora of fruits, meats, and vegetables, some she recognized and some were just as strange as the Vigilo trailing her steps. She started piling a little of everything on her plate.

"Hungry?" asked a light, amused voice. Verity laughed and turned to the pale, petite Fae woman beside her. The Fae's hair was long and the lightest blond. She had part of it braided like a crown around her head and the rest hung loosely down her back.

"I just want to try it all," Verity answered, "then I'll know what I want next time."

The light voice tinkled a laugh though it was soft and somehow warm. Verity had an instant affection for the lady.

"Have you been here long?" Verity asked her.

"Oh, yes, I grew up here," the Fae said as she selected a bright green turnip looking vegetable and took a small bite before selecting a few more items, holding them in her hand rather than using a plate.

As they moved away from the food, the Fae lady gestured to a nearby table. Sitting down, Verity questioned, "Would it be rude of me to ask where you fit in, in all this?"

"Possibly," the women replied, "but I don't mind."

Verity chuckled. "Oh good. The last thing I need is to offend the wrong person."

"That might be true, but we all suspect you are higher on the hierarchy than most of us and wouldn't presume to do anything to prompt our Queen's wrath." The woman looked around before leaning toward Verity. "She is a Queen of consequence and will not hesitate to do the right thing even if distasteful."

Verity frowned as she savored an oddly shaped pink fruit. She wasn't sure if that meant the Queen would be rude and throw people into dungeons as needed or if she would tear them limb from limb like a Viking. She decided not to clarify it for the moment.

"I'm Verity Applebee," she told her new friend.

"I know." The lady smiled. "I think most do now. I'm Brihana from the west of Bennen."

"What does that mean exactly?"

Brihana pressed her lips together in an amused smile. "It means that supposedly I am from the west nether regions of my father Bennen."

Verity choked on a weedy purple grass-like vegetable. She forced the disgusting thing down before laughing.

"I apologize," Verity said when she'd calmed. "But I did not expect that."

The lady grinned and patted Verity on the shoulder. "I know and you have no idea how long I have waited to tell someone."

They were interrupted by a young Fae girl with a rainbow of colors inked on her long slender ears. The girl gave a partial bow to Verity before saying, "The Queen wishes to visit with you this evening for late supper. She will send someone for you when the time is right."

"Thank you," Verity replied and watched the girl skip away before turning back to Brihana.

"That's quite an honor," Brihana commented as she dropped the last of the food from her palm into her mouth. "Until then, would you like me to show you some of the things we do to occupy our time? Beading, sewing, herbing?"

"I would enjoy that," Verity told her new friend and brushed off her hands as she stood.

"Wonderful! A change in my day is most welcome."

They moved together to leave the field.

"I hadn't thought the Fae did those sorts of things," Verity commented as they stepped onto a path and veered left. Brihana laughed softly.

"What, sewing? We pride ourselves in our fabric, our clothing, and our hair." She shook her head and the long pale locks moved like silk down her back.

Verity smiled. She had made a friend, she was going to try her medically oriented hands at embroidery and she was meeting the Queen, who was somehow her relation, for dinner. Oh, and she had an invisible dog trailing her.

Chapter 17

Liam's lips drew into a broad smile that lit up the room when he saw Andy. It was Liam who had found Andy, a runaway foster kid trying to figure out why he was different. For Liam, it was like finding a lost member of the family. Both Andy and Sloane had been lost souls for a while back then and coming together had helped them both. They had been bantering like siblings ever since, making Liam secretly happy to have been there from the beginning.

They exchanged a man hug when Liam finally reached him. They were meeting the Queen and Liam hadn't expected to see Andy, a student, hanging out with the big bads. Sloane was trailing behind him chatting with a little blond gnome lady whose name Liam could never remember.

"It's so good to see you," Andy said, his eyes shining with excitement.

"Missed you, bro." Liam slapped Andy on the arm. "What are you doing up here?"

"It's a surprise." Andy beamed. Liam laughed.

"Andy!" Sloane's voice boomed around the room causing several people to look up from their desks. Sloane blushed. "So sorry," she muttered from behind her hand. Then she turned back to

Andy and threw her arms out, giving him a bear hug of champions. Andy laughed and Liam felt a little more warmth fill his heart. He frowned and fisted himself in the chest a couple of times. He still wasn't used to the amount of joy he could get out of things. It was weird.

The Queen's secretary Joy slithered away from her desk and joined them with a smile that would chill any man's bones. Liam was no exception. Her sharp teeth could easily lacerate any flesh except maybe a changed gargoyle.

"The Queen should be here any moment," she told them, her lisp as strong as ever.

"Thank you." Sloane blinked furiously at Liam and then at Andy. Andy got the hint first.

"Joy, this is Sloane McDougall. Sloane, this is Joy."

Joy held out a hand and Sloane took it with a broad smile.

"Please to meet you!" Sloane beamed. "Are you some type of gorgon?"

It was Liam's turn to blink and raise his brows at his wife, who completely ignored him.

"Why yes, dear!" Joy seemed pleased. She pointed with a chuckle at her short brown hair. "Of course, no snakes. You know your mythology."

Sloane shrugged but her eyes were sparkling. "I don't generally remember much of it but the more I encounter in real life, the faster it comes back to me."

The lady patted her on the arm. "Ah, here she is," Joy said and turned toward the glass office where Sloane watched a huge gargoyle came in through the patio door, wave and then go behind a dainty folded wall. Sloane took in a breath.

"I thought you'd seen her in form before," Liam mentioned softly, placing a hand on Sloane's back. Sloane shook her head.

"I seem to miss her at every turn. What a beautiful sight."

Liam squeezed her waist gently before heading into the office just as the Queen came from behind the wall dressed in a soft pink business suit with beige heels and smiling broadly. Liam dipped at the waist.

"My Queen," he said.

"Welcome back, Liam. I am glad you and Sloane were able to come." She gestured for Sloane to come closer. Andy followed at her heel. Sloane took the Queen's proffered hand. The queen put her other hand on top enclosing Sloane's and gave a small squeeze before releasing her. She nodded at Andy in greeting.

"Please, have a seat." She waved to the chairs in front of her desk.

The Director breezed into the room and closed the door behind him. Liam watched the Queen meet his eyes and the warmth there was oddly comforting. The Queen turned to Sloane.

"I appreciate you're okay with Liam's *partial* retirement from the Den," she remarked. Sloane chuckled.

"If he's anything like me, he would either go nuts without the Den or he would drive me nuts."

The room laughed, breaking the small tension that had settled in. The Queen folded her hands in front of her and looked at each of them individually before speaking again.

"Andy has already been briefed. I am sure you are curious about his attendance here, as I would be. He is still a student but, on this mission, his skills will be invaluable. As far as I know there are only three Displacer's left in this world."

Andy shivered. Liam stiffened. Sloane glanced around the room. He thought she understood the meaning but maybe not the consequence. The Director moved to stand by the Queen. It was then Sloane realized the Director was human. She had simply assumed he was a Guardian.

"There are many, many styles of Guardians," he explained. "The Displacer was rare, yes, but not so much so that attention was put on it. Over the last few we have lost many Displacers to various accidents and because they were lost over such a long period of time, it wasn't until recently we realized the dwindling number and started to get the idea they weren't always accidents."

"That being said," the Queen picked up the story. "I want a Displacer on this mission. The other two are on crucial missions of their own and could not be spared although," she paused as concern flickered in her eyes as she gazed upon Andy, "if anything happens during this mission, they will be reassigned to this case."

She stood.

"It will be dangerous. There are far more things I don't know than what I do know. I would go myself except I believe..."

"And I know is true," the Director inserted.

The Queen gave him a dark look which he ignored. She continued.

"I believe it would put me in grave danger and without my protege, things would change. Drastically. I don't know if the Den would ever recover."

There was a stunned silence for a moment before Sloane let out a low whistle. Liam cleared his throat.

"What is the mission?" he asked.

"I need you to find my protege. I know her general location. I know she is shielded, and it barely allows the periodic entrance of my sight."

"So, she's gone through the change then?" Liam questioned.

"I don't think so, not yet. She has connected though. Her tethers have set but her location has somehow been hidden. I've felt her a few times in the last year. Connor and Tio were the ones who died finding her location. When this mess is over, we will have a reward ceremony for their valor. I am indebted to them both for their find."

The Queen rubbed her face as thought she had a headache. "Liam, you are team leader. You have Andy and I encourage you to get a team together of at least six more. It is imperative you bring the Princess back. The Director will fill you in with the details that we have. I would like you to prepare your team and launch in the next couple of days."

"Yes, ma'am," Liam said as he stood and bowed.

"What about me?" Sloane asked.

The Queen looked at Liam. He was about to tell

Sloane she would need to stay here with the Queen during the mission.

"It will be dangerous," the Queen stated. "The consequences of you going are unknown, Sloane. But your innate skills could come in handy."

Liam pressed him lips together.

Sloane stood straighter. "I want to help. I'll go." Her glare dared Liam to deny her. He had but one weakness.

"Liam?" The Queen's face was grim as their eyes met. "You must move forward with extreme caution."

Chapter 18

It had been almost a year since Lauren had started feeling the pulse in her skin. It was like a million spots all over her skin that pointed to something she could only think of as souls. It helped her stay positive. It kept her above the dirt and lost lives. The points felt close though she had no idea who or what they were. There were lines that led out from the points but she didn't know how to connect them. It was gray and hazy.

"Child, are you listening?"

Lauren met her teacher's eyes. They were old and red. A goblin if she recalled correctly. A crotchety, mean one too.

"Yes, teacher."

"What did I say. And speak carefully, I've no patience for your antics today."

Lauren squirmed in her seat. She had not, in fact, been listening. And Teacher's lack of patience hurt.

"I apologize, I wasn't listening at that moment, but I did have attention on something you said earlier. You had said depending on the type, size, and moisture levels, there were varying chances of mud slides during a heavy storm. Could you elaborate?"

FOUND

The Teacher blinked his big ugly eyes and a gray tongue licked one of the two long teeth that hung from the incredibly large mouth. The Teacher smiled. It was frightening and Lauren did her best to not jump from her seat.

"Now that is an interesting question, for once."

And off Teacher went into more talk about dirt. Lauren fought the desire to moan in frustration. She was still nursing the bruise on her arm from the last time she had pissed off Teacher, but she also needed to know about dirt. Her plan required it.

As the Teacher spoke in earnest about her new favorite subject, Lauren's arm dangled beside her chair. She twirled her finger around and watched as the dirt in the corner of the room danced in a graceful spiral.

Lauren smiled.

Chapter 19

Andy sat in Liam's living room drinking from a teacup shaped liked a dragon and watching Liam catch up with old friends. Sloane was busy in the kitchen, making coffee and tea, serving cupcakes and finger foods, and generally taking care of the growing number of visitors in her home.

Kam, who had been working with Liam for years on various adventures, was bent over with laughter while the siren, Andy thought her name started with a Z, stood nearby and watched with her nose crinkled in distaste.

Evan Smith had arrived an hour prior. He had been part of the small war that had brought down Sloane's father-in-law and ended the insane quest to create a perfect society where there were *no monsters*. It was ironic seeing as how the man had ended up being a monster himself.

Sloane had lost her mother that day. She'd almost lost Liam but he had an uncanny ability of not being able to die which saved him from that fate. Evan looked a bit worse for wear. It was odd since the times Andy had seen him, he seemed a cheerful fellow if a bit reserved. Andy knew he was similar, and it was okay with him. He was happy with himself and with his life. He was sad about his parents, but it had been so long and having found this new clan, he could put his past behind him and be okay.

You okay, man? He wanted to ask Evan who stood near the window and watched the waves lap against the sea wall. At least that's what it looked like. Andy couldn't decide what to do when Evan turned to him.

"I haven't found Verity yet," he mumbled but Andy heard him perfectly.

"What?" Andy asked. It was the first he'd heard anything about Verity. He was surprised Evan was talking to him about it.

"Verity was taken. By a *Fae,"* he sneered, surprising Andy further, "and I couldn't do a thing. *I was literally frozen*. That was weeks ago. I still can't find her. I came on this mission hoping to clear my head before I go searching again."

"I'm sorry to hear that," Andy said. He blinked a few times and then looked around the room at anything other than Evan who was acting about as in character as a turtle dancing like a tree nymph.

The doorbell rang. And again and again.

Liam gave a good-natured holler. He seemed to be in his element. Evan backed up and stared out the window again. Liam opened the door and greeted someone. Andy couldn't quite see with Kam and the siren in the way. Then he heard a laugh and bolted from his seat.

Brick!

Andy met Brick with a bear hug before he

could get a second step through the doorway. Brick laughed and hugged him back. Andy pulled away and couldn't stop grinning at the man who had taken him in like a son, prepped him for the Guardian school and had his back like the Dad he hadn't had in far too long.

"How's my boy?" Brick asked. His voice boomed throughout the house.

"Gah!" Sloane hollered. "Talk a little louder Brick!"

The man laughed. "Hi, Sloane," he said in the exact same volume he had before. She growled but everyone knew it was in jest.

"Well?" He looked at Andy. "How are you?"

"I'm..." Andy cocked his head and drew his lips to one side. "Okay despite everything." Brick nodded.

"Good." He slapped Andy on the back, never a man for more words than necessary, and with Andy headed toward the kitchen.

Liam opened the door yet again and smiled broadly at Dustin Abernathy. They man hugged and as they pulled away, two more people entered the house. Liam was surprised.

"Who invited this asshole to the party?" he hollered, his lips quirking at the sides. Simon and Sheba stood holding hands.

"I believe you did, wimp," the small lady said.

"Simon and Sheba, welcome to my home," Liam greeted them. "Simon, I am ever so glad you were extremely unhelpful in teaching me to break the bond."

Simon raised his hand, Sheba's clasped gently

within. "When it's good, it's great."

"You can say that again." Liam gestured to the kitchen. "There's drinks and snacks in the kitchen. We'll give a brief and then go from there. Glad to have you on board."

He turned to Dustin. "And you too, my friend. Really glad to have you with me on this one."

Surprise moved over Dustin's face but before he could answer, Sloane saw him and screamed. The other Guardian's frowned as the high pitch was not a normal sound coming from anyone in this house, but there it was piercing their ears. Sloane ran over and launched herself into Dustin's arms. He hugged her tight and Andy knew it was complete trust that kept Liam from pulling her away and knocking Dustin's head from his neck.

Sloane dragged Dustin to the kitchen to get him fueled up while she chattered away.

Andy popped a third or maybe a tenth cookie into his mouth and looked around the room. Some people he knew well and considered family. Some he'd met and some were brand new. He wondered about the couple that had arrived. He let out a contented sigh. This was his life. It was different, it was weird, and things were always changing but he had a place in it that was all his.

That place was with these people, living an adventure and saving the world one day at a time.

Chapter 20

During the enlightening visit with Brihana and two other Fae ladies who were also not shy, Verity found herself grossly inadequate in the field of embroidery and beading. When she finished torturing herself, she went back to her room and cleaned up. There was a beautiful emerald green gown in the closet and she pulled it on and posed in the mirror.

She looked like a fairy princess. She laughed and twirled. It wasn't her choice for daily wear but for an evening out, she'd take it. She was getting more used to wearing colors and moving further away from her usual black. It suited her love of sparkly things even if it wasn't in her comfort zone. She wouldn't have minded some eyeliner and mascara though. She raised her hand and with a flourish, imagined the thick black lines of coal around her eyes. She smiled as her imagination created the exact lines she envisioned. It was her best makeup ever.

Blinking and expecting the vision to vanish, Verity felt a rush of blood in her head when she realized the makeup was actually on her face. She felt the mascara on her lashes and blinked again. She wanted to test this strange new ability further but didn't want to do something stupid like ruin a perfectly beautiful gown. A giggle caught in her throat as she twirled once more. She was acting like royalty and it didn't feel right or normal but it sure was fun. She glanced at the door wondering how late a late dinner was and how long she would have before someone came and collected her.

She settled herself in a comfortable chair near the bed to wait. As she stared absently at the door her mind wandered for the first time since her arrival. So many things had surprised her and left her spinning she had forgotten the rest of the world for a time.

She thought of her parents. They had never let on she was anything other than their daughter in every way possible. They loved her, she had no doubt, so perhaps they too had never known of the deceit of the Fae. Not really deceit she supposed, but she didn't have a good enough grasp on what to expect to really know how to feel about any of it.

She thought of Evan then and stilled for a moment. He was special, caring, and thoughtful. He wanted her. She had felt the odd strings of the Guardian bond working through his hands, his kiss...

A loud knock startled Evan's face from her mind. She blinked at the door. The knock came again. She had no doubt who was behind it. With a sigh, she stood and shook out her skirts. She opened the door and found Duran standing with his back to her, hands clasped behind his back. He didn't move as she shut the door behind her and went to his side.

"Verity," he said with a nod and started walking. He was in a strange mood, quiet and actually walked at a speed she could keep up with. She felt no need to be conversant either. She recalled her last moment with Evan. Only a few days ago and yet it was another lifetime. Verity had been so eager to jump into a relationship with someone. With anyone, it seemed, that looked at her twice. But now? She wanted to explore and find her true self. Discover her abilities and put them to work with her passion to help.

"Hm," Verity commented to herself. It was a startling realization but one that oddly pleased her. She felt calm and ready to learn, like a sponge. A light current of power moved through her core. She took Duran's arm to stabilize herself, continuing to walk with him but her head was slightly bent, eyes closed while she experienced the power settling. When it reached her extremities and settled, she sighed and opened her eyes. Letting go of Duran she shook out her hands.

"You're close," Duran observed. Verity nodded.

"I think tomorrow, in the morning after breakfast, you should take me to your girl."

Duran lowered his head slightly in response. He offered his arm again and Verity took it as they walked up the path to the Queen's Faerie Castle. It was old, cracked, and covered in thick green vines, but still magnificent.

FOUND

Verity had not noticed it before, but she wasn't surprised at its appearance during the walk. She was coming to understand the reason the Fae were so sporadic in behavior and thus feared was because their power was to the individual's choice. What one wanted to occur, they simply made occur. Understanding of anything further was beyond Verity's grasp but the simplistic view and process of decision was not. It made so much sense that she couldn't help but wonder why humans were so stunted in their spiritual nature. She thought deeper and wondered if it was better kept that way. She shook the thought away. She knew in her heart most humans were good and beautiful people who just wanted to live and to take pleasure in their life. It was the ones who sought only to destroy who made the human world so difficult. As long as there were people who enjoyed suffering, the human world would suffer.

Verity brought her head up high. More now than ever, she wanted to help. She had grown up in the human world and still called it home. At that moment, Verity knew it would always be her home and she would leave the Fae lands as soon as her business here was concluded.

The gates at the main entrance were tall enough to let an elephant through. They opened as the two neared and closed quietly behind them. The interior was a colorful courtyard with purple grass, black and white flowers and a multicolored sky.

Duran led her through several immaculately decorated hallways and rooms before they came to a stop at Victorian style double doors. He looked at her, eyebrows raised before pushing through them.

The room Verity walked into was reminiscent of the Earth days of grandeur. She pondered how the Fae determined what was fashionable. The heavy wooden dining table was long enough to hold at least twenty people. The wall at the far end of the room was painted brilliantly in the colors of a peacock. The scene similar to a Monet. It featured part of a lily pond and a dock with several well-dressed people looking over the pond, and a duck floated in the background. Verity went to turn away when one of the people on the dock moved away from the others. Duran went to sit at the long table with a grunt. Verity watch avidly as the figure in the painting walked slowly down the beach toward her.

Verity pulled her head back when she came face to face with the Queen in the painting. The Queen smiled and stepped out.

"Wow," Verity exhaled. The Queen only waved a hand at the seat next to hers at the end. Duran had already seated himself in the one next to Verity.

Rothald entered the room then. His paleness was both accentuated and improved by the stiff blue suit.

"Mother, Duran, Miss Verity." He bowed to his mother and quickly sat in the other chair next to her. Verity had noticed it before, but the final piece clicked in her mind at this. To her memory, the eldest, not the youngest was closest to the head. But then again, it was usually a King or a Lord that would have the head, not a Queen, so what did she know. She glanced at Duran and he didn't seem bothered by it, so she brought her eyes back to the Queen.

For the next two hours they made small talk and ate enough food to feed New York City. Verity rubbed her swollen belly and was quietly thankful for the lack of a corset. Verity was done with the facade and just wanted to get Duran's girl seen to and leave this place. She really wanted to know about her parentage but at the same time, she wasn't sure that she did. Before she could decide whether to ask, the Queen rested her elbow on the table, put a smug cheek to her palm and winked at Verity.

The room changed. Gone was the table and the painting. With a glance, Verity realized they were *in* the painting. They all sat, still in their chairs, on the beach of the very pond in the picture. The duck quacked from across the water and from the dark green brush four ducklings swam out. They surrounded their mother and went about on a tour of the pond. The low voices of men came from the dock where several stood pulling on cigars. The musty scent wafted near in the light breeze. Verity smiled and nodded at the Queen.

"Well played," she said. The Queen laughed.

"I just love that trick," the Queen replied before the joy drained from her face. Verity realized suddenly the boys were uncharacteristically quiet. She looked over and they both sat still as boards, the life seemingly vacant. They looked to have become part of the immobile painting where everything else had come alive. A chill dripped down her back, settling cold and stiff in her bones.

"I used to play hide and seek in here with her," the Queen lamented. Verity shifted in her seat and cleared her throat.

"Who exactly?"

"Your mother."

The chill became a tidal wave in Verity's nerves. She stayed quiet, assimilating, and trying to evaluate the importance.

"My sister was kinder, and had more love inside," the Queen continued. The chills turned to fire in Verity's neck. While the Queen was lost in thought, Verity glanced at the two sons. Rothald's eyes were wide with fear yet he was silent and still in his painting form. Duran, however, had managed to solidify one arm and was reaching for Verity. She took the hint. She hadn't done it before, but it was time for her to try her first vanishing act.

The Queen turned to her then.

"You look just like her, you know. She was the picture of our father. As the rightful..." The Queen became distracted by something occurring behind Verity.

Knowing that what the Queen was about to say was probably only for the ears of the soon-to-be-dead, Verity bolted from her chair and stepped into the air.

A rush of wind accosted her senses as she fell through the nothingness. She forced her mind to replay her destination over and over while consciously trying not to panic. All the while, a tinkling laugh filled her mind. As her feet hit solid ground and her body crashed into something solid, she heard the Queen's voice reverberating in her mind.

"Until we meet again, little fairy."

Chapter 21

Instead of taking a Faeway or a commercial airline, the rescue crew flew on a private jet. It seemed large, and Andy guessed it held about forty people. Which meant that for the eight plus hour haul from Florida to Dublin, people could separate and spread comfortably about the plane.

Dustin, Brick, Evan, and Zarra, Andy was finally reminded of her name even though everyone else called her Jaws, played a game of Poker. Liam, Sloane, and Kam were catching up. Simon and Sheba were napping while Andy played a dragon fighting game on his phone. An hour into the flight, a familiar shiver crossed his shoulders and he looked up to see Charlese materialize in the seat across from him.

"You're getting quite good at that," he commented, a smile playing at the corners of his lips. She smiled and it lit a fire in his heart.

Mine.

The thought crossed his mind and he had an inkling of what Liam had gone through not so long ago.

"Why thank you," she answered and adjusted herself in the seat to be more comfortable. "It's getting easier and easier. The second Elder believes I have a special gift in essence travel."

"That's because you instinctively knew you needed extra skill to follow me around the globe."

"Ha ha," Charlese said as she glanced around the plane. Apparently, whatever she saw pleased her as she smiled broadly and stood, moving to drop herself onto Andy's lap. He was surprised but not bothered with the action. Not. At. All. She put an arm around his shoulder, and he placed a hand on her hip. She was warm as though she was truly there with him.

"Wow, you are exceptionally good at this," he whispered.

"Told you." She brought her lips to his. It was hesitant at first but then they found their rhythm and it was a zapping and zinging of nerves, and his body became very excited with her apparent nearness. She pulled away.

"Goodness, you're tasty," she teased. Andy smiled. She lowered her head slightly and looked him over, running a finger down his cheek that left his nerves tingling in its wake.

"See you again soon," she whispered as she faded away.

Andy sat, staring at nothing, feeling her warmth seep away and his body settle back down. He shook his head. What he would do to just have her near him, in the flesh, all the time.

Chapter 22

The moment she had laid eyes on Andrew Chamberlain, Charlese Campbell knew.

That was despite the fact that only once had she been able to touch Andy with her bare hands. The school dance had turned from merely an entertaining evening to the catch of a lifetime. If his creature had known they were a matched pair, it hadn't made it evident.

But she knew. Time and some true face to face smooches would close the deal she was sure.

He was magic and light and the perfect addition to her white witch ways. She wondered if he was both her true mate and her familiar in one. It could happen she supposed.

"Charlese."

Pulled from her interesting line of thought, Charlese looked up. She met the eyes of her teacher, Mrs. Beirinhauf.

"Yes, Ma'am?"

"Please state the two berries that are deadly to the pixie fae."

"Holly and Blue."

The teacher watched her thoughtfully for a moment before nodding.

FOUND

Charlese sat at the school desk in the last hour of the last year of her textbook schooling and drew lazy circles on her notebook while her teacher droned on about the magic system of the pixie fae. For some reason Mrs. Beirinhauf thought actual teaching was required during this last class even if it was review.

Glancing at the clock, again, Charlese gritted her teeth. Agonizing. She already knew the three levels of pixie forms, just like the human card game come to think of it. She drew a lightning bolt. She already knew the ages, the power levels. She already knew the magics to ward them when they were too annoying or dangerous.

Potion class was more interesting. The hands on work was hard but rewarding. Despite her photographic mind, getting the amounts and ingredients perfect was a challenge.

But her absolute favorite was essence travel. She had mastered levels that most graduates only wished for. She was better than her teacher and catching up to her idol, The White Witch of the Salt Lakes. At least that is what her teacher said.

Seeing Andy during her walks was the bonus. A large one. She contemplated when she would have the opportunity to visit him again when the gong boomed throughout the hall indicating the end of the school day. The class whooped; Charlese included.

After a well-earned two month break at home with family, though calling that a break was misleading, her apprenticeship would begin.

She had not chosen her favorite witch, who resided in the states, but had decided to apprentice with Babe Lent in France. Maybe not her favorite but talented in the ways that Charlese needed to continue her education. With a smile, Charlese curled her finger in her hair. Being in France would keep her near the one person she wanted to be around even more than the famous white witch.

Andrew Chamberlain.

FOUND

Chapter 23

By the time the plane landed and they had come together at the Dublin den, Andy had played several games of poker, napped, written a poem for Charlese which he promptly threw away and eaten a pound of European chocolate. With Sloane and Liam. They were a terrible influence when it came to chocolate and ice cream.

It was early morning, daylight still a couple of hours away and he was bored. The time change had him off kilter. He left the Den with a nod to one of the local guardians and took to the streets of Dublin for a walk. He walked along the River Liffey admiring the old buildings and breathing the salty air. Something about it spoke to him.

He paused at the Ha'penny Bridge, then walked halfway across it and stopped to soak it all in.

One moment he was sighing in contentment and the next, something akin to a building hit his head with a crack. His stomach twisted and his head spun before he hit the cement.

Chapter 24

Grabbing her toothbrush, Lauren jammed it into her mouth and fell onto her bed. She bit down hard. She normally would have been concerned about breaking her teeth but today it was all about protecting herself from being found out. Moaning softly, she ground her teeth as she tried so hard to stop the pain.

A thought wiggled its way through.

Release.

Her head throbbed, her back felt like it was being burned and stabbed and her hands? The bones shifted beneath the skin. She could *see* it. She shuddered.

Release.

Again, the word sifted through the aching and finally made its way into her thick skull. Lauren rolled off the bed and onto the rug below. On all fours, she forced herself to stop fighting, to welcome the pain. It was so hard.

Finally, something happened. The toothbrush dropped to the ground. Her body started to move in a push and pull of fluid motions. It tingled with change, in a blood rushed mess of nerves. And then she was different, but the same. She sat back on her heels and instantly pulled away after poking herself in the bum. She glanced at her feet.

"What the..." she whispered to herself, startled by the strange gruff inflection in her normally soft voice. Looking at the door, she waited for someone to rush in and capture her. She waited a full minute and when the door stayed closed, she stood and smiled around the strange sensation of a different mouth. Her teeth felt huge, and sharp too. She blinked a few times and noticed the significant changes in her vision. Crisper, cleaner.

A flash of power came out of nowhere and slammed into her chest. Lauren fell back onto the bed. It creaked loudly beneath her weight and all the spots on her skin flared to life, thousands of points of awareness that came alive and then, nothing. The life that had flashed hope in her chest was snuffed out. The tiny lifelines around her hushed to their soft hum.

Lauren found her body back in its usual human form. She lay down and pulled up her comforter over her naked body just as her door swung open and hit the wall.

Byram, Marten's favorite guard stared at her accusingly.

"What happened?" he demanded.

"What are you talking about? Trying to get comfortable here."

He snarled and stared at her another moment before he left, leaving her door open. She knew better than to close it. The result would simply hurt.

But her plan had just gotten a whole lot better.

Chapter 25

Andy couldn't explain it. He had been standing on the bridge, and then he was waking up.

The pounding in his temple was the first thing Andy noted as he started to be aware once more. He felt strange, like he was floating in space. It had been so long since he had stepped foot in water denser than a shower he could only guess he felt submerged.

He took in a deep breath and it felt strange. The air seemed to fill his head and neck like a bubbling champagne before feeding the rest of his body. It helped his head tremendously however, so he took in several more deep breathes. He felt thick and heavy and the air was a smooth and cool relief. The sensation of bubbles tickled his nose.

Andy's eyes slammed open. His heart just about came out of throat as his abrupt motion scared away the fish inspecting his nose. He blinked several times. And then he panicked. Thrashing his body, he tried to flail his arms but they were trapped behind his back and his feet were tied to something heavy. When he realized he needed to just stop and look, he saw the world around him was thick with life.

He stretched his neck back and could see the

glimmer of sunlight shining into the water above. Looking at the ground below him, sea creatures made their way along the sand. Crabs, shrimp, bottom feeding fish and to his left, a huge section of algae was casting an eerie green glow.

Breathing in again, he felt the water as it flowed into his nose and mouth, the cool bubbles tickling his nasal passages and despite his predicament he felt himself smile. He released a calming exhale and watched the bubbles flow outward. He frowned as bubbles hit the back of his neck, rolling over his shoulder and joining his exhale. A chill rent down his back. Did he have company?

Focusing on his hands he tried to feel what had them bound. He quickly determined that he was no escape artist and shifted his arms, the dark swirls of the change blending with the blue-black of the water around him. The restraints snapped. He quickly twisted to look behind and saw nothing except rippling waters, fish, and algae. He shook out his arms before bending to inspect the situation at his feet. He laughed after startling a school of passing fish.

Then he shook his head and laughed some more. He was friggin breathing under water! He would have stomped and maybe even danced if he had more of an idea of what in the holy heck had happened and also the use of his feet.

They were wrapped several times by a thick rope that looked like it might have come from a ship's riggings. The rope was then looped into what looked like a huge old wagon wheel. He tugged on it but it barely budged. Making the shift from human to gargoyle, he broke the rope and stepped away from the trap. A normal person would be dead right now.

Like his parents. He remembered the Queen's story about his mother. Hesitantly, he reached up to his neck. As soon as he felt them, he pulled away. Then he took a cleansing breath, shook the tension from his arms and neck and reached up again.

Gills.

He had GILLS!

Blowing out, bubbles left his nose, mouth and gills. The rush of oxygen and strength of adrenaline shot through him. He couldn't wait to tell Charlese.

Of course, that would be after he got out of here and figured out where here was, what had happened and then got back to his team.

He looked up at the water's edge. He guessed it was about twenty feet high. Andy wondered if his captors were still up there somewhere. How had he been dropped in the middle of what appeared to be a deep lake before he had time to wake? Guardians healed pretty darn quickly. A hit to the head might take a little longer but not that long. He wondered why they hadn't just removed his head. That would assure them of his death. Something tickled his mind and he couldn't quite grasp what was bothering him about this picture.

He felt his stomach lurch and the fact the crab cruising nearby looked tasty told him he needed to get a move on. Just before he bent his legs to push off to the surface, he saw them. Four bodies emerged from behind a sunken plant and algae covered sailboat with a bite shaped hole in its hull. They swam toward him. Andy waited. The likelihood of these beings hurting him was pretty low he thought, or rather hoped. He frowned as he watched them come closer when he remembered one of these creatures had somehow removed him from a bridge, tied him up and dunked him here without him having any idea it was happening.

The four creatures came to float before him. Andy's weight in gargoyle form made it easy for him to stand in the silt of the lake. The gills were still fluttering at his neck and he reveled in the odd sensation even as he took in these ethereal beings. They seemed to float with no effort, their inky skin blended in the surroundings though the strength of their spirits resonated in the water around them. Each held a weapon of a sorts, a long, sharpened bone, individually carved and sharped.

Eelfae.

Andy slowly lifted a clawed hand and waved. One of them, a lady he gathered by the long dark hair tied behind her head, smiled. Stark white teeth with razor fine edges glittered before vanishing. One of the males frowned but it only made the lady smile again. She seemed... Andy watched her before he decided. She seemed excited, giddy almost. She opened her mouth as if to speak and a series of clicks, chirps and grunts surrounded him. Andy shook his head and the lady eelfae looked saddened. One of the males pointed toward the shore and Andy nodded. Cautious, he stayed in gargoyle form and swam awkwardly to the indicated shoreline. The eelfae zoomed ahead. When he finally trudged up the muck and sand of the shore, they stood nearby. In the early morning light, the men looked quite dark, but the lady had similar coloring to his own, dark but more a coffee brown with a little cream. She had long dark hair plated in the back. There were pearls in a strand around her neck. One of the men had orange streaks in his hair. Andy wondered if that was similar to the graying of a human. Another man had his hair cut close but choppy, like he just cut off hunks when it grew too long. The last man had hair reaching to his shoulder blades. It was held back by what looked like a ribbon but since the man had a necklace made out of what very much resembled bones, but Andy was pretty sure he didn't want to know what the hair ribbon was made up of exactly. They were all wrapped snuggly in some kind of seaweed looking material. It reminded Andy of the leotards and flowing outfits worn by ballet dancers.

The lady smiled again, and he saw her hands rubbing together nervously. An idea struck him.

"I'm going to change," he told them, as he shifted one claw into a hand while pointing at it with the other. Two of the men nodded, and one answered with a gravelly sounding yes.

Andy shifted his upper body but kept his form on the lower. He didn't have any clothes to put on and considering all four of them were draped in their seaweed looking clothing, he didn't know how much they might care about such things.

Three of them stood together while the fourth, the one with the chunked-out hair, stood further back, his weapon at the ready, watching everything around them. A guard, Andy surmised.

He walked toward the female and held out his hand. She placed hers on his without delay. He smiled and pulled it closer so he could look at the lines, the coloring and her nails. He looked at his own. Then he turned to the male with the orange streaks. The lady spoke again, the clicks and grunts so loud it was almost painful. She grimaced and tried again, lowering her voice. But the sounds still meant nothing to him. Andy looked at the male who then nodded and held out a hand. The color was different, the nail bed was more like a claw than a human fingernail. But hers, hers was like Andy's.

"I speak some English, Guardian," the scary bone wearing man told him with a guttural slur, "you learn too." Andy didn't really follow his meaning but smiled at the man who seemed placated by the gesture.

The lady became impatient and clapped her hands. When she met Andy's gaze, she pointed at herself.

"Sissa," she ground out.

"Okay," Andy acknowledged and gave a dubious smile. Was that her name, he wondered? He pointed at himself and spoke, "Andy."

The lady frowned and he could tell she was

thinking hard. Just as Andy got a sudden itch to leave this place and find his team, she huffed out a breath and pointed at Andy.

"Brotha," she stated and smiled proudly as she folded her arms over her chest. Andy's mouth dropped open. The lady laughed and then pointed to the long-haired male who spoke English. "Brotha," she said. She pointed at herself.

"Sissa," and then she pointed to Andy, "Brotha." He closed his mouth, but his eyes widened.

The male who had shook his hand earlier, the one with the orange streaks, stepped forward and pointed to himself. "Uncle," he announced clearly.

Feelings, tingles just below the surface of his skin erupted behind Andy's ears and flowed down his arms and legs. He looked over each of the strange creatures before him. He compared eyes, cheekbones, ears, body structure and skin. And suddenly these creatures didn't seem so strange. It felt right. It felt better than right.

"Family," he whispered trying not to allow the sting in his eyes to develop into something mushy.

"Family," his uncle echoed.

"Family," his sister repeated though she glanced at her brother for what he thought was clarification.

"How did you get here?" Andy held out his arms and at that moment finally realized his surroundings.

The sandy beach, rocks and thick brush around them were all out in the open. A human could show up at any time. Back to reality, he worried about being half-shifted. He worried about his team and he was star struck at being found by his new eelfae family.

"Long story," his Uncle said. He pointed to Andy's head. "Sorry for…" he paused and apparently not finding the appropriate word, made a punching motion toward his own head.

Any damage Andy had received when his Uncle had knocked him out was gone so he just waved a hand and smiled. His Uncle gave a stern nod. They obviously had known exactly who he was when they took him otherwise, he could have died. Andy frowned and decided not to go down that path of questions.

"I must go," Andy told them, "but I want to learn. I want to know everything." His Uncle translated to his sister. Her mouth turned down, but she kept repeating *yes.*

"This," his scary brother said while he gestured around them, "is Lough Liffey near Valleymount. Come in two weeks. Your mover is there." The man pointed and Andy could see a jeep like vehicle across the river. He nodded and looked at his sister. She walked over and stood in front of him. They had the same almond shaped brown eyes he noticed. She reached out and squeezed his arm before walking around him and started toward the water. The others followed her, and he watched them vanish into the lake before noticing one of them had left their weapon behind.

Andy took it and started the walk to the vehicle, hoping it had a GPS. And clothes.

Chapter 26

Verity pulled herself up from the floor and found herself in her old room. She had crashed into her chest of drawers at home. Despite her fear of being followed, a rush of excitement rent through her spine as she realized the truth of her new powers.

She glanced around the room. It hadn't changed since she'd left just a few years ago. She'd been so eager to pursue her nursing dreams and make it on her own. Her own apartment was small but comfortable and though she missed her parents and dropped in to see them from time to time, it was her safe place.

Her parents.

Sinking down on her bed, Verity breathed in the familiar smell of home. Despite what the Queen said, her parents loved her like their own and Verity didn't think they knew any different.

She stood and went to the door, listening. A deep mumble made her smile. Her father. She cracked the door and looked out. She could hear them from the living room, or her dad at least. The television was on in the background, just like it always was. Creeping down the hallway Verity slowed as she neared the living room. She peered around the corner and watched as her mom handed her father a plate piled high with a sandwich before sitting down beside him with her own plate on her lap. He picked up the sandwich and after swallowing his first bite thanked her mom for lunch. Just like he always did.

She rubbed a finger over her lips as she thought about the supposed deception of her birth. It just didn't feel right, and Verity didn't believe it. They had no idea.

She watched a moment more as her mom leaned back, pulling a book from the side table and settling in next to her dad as he watched his shows. Then she turned and stepped into the air.

This time she landed with a thud on the hard ground, and fell to her knees. She wondered how long it took to get the hang of Fae travel as she got to her feet. Walking toward the door, she glanced around the room she'd slept in during her earlier visit at the Goblin's Lair. She cracked it and peered into the outer chamber, a smaller bedroom for a maid or guard. It was empty so she made her way to the exit into the hallway. At the door, she listened hard while breathing in the sweet air. It was alive, like a healthy garden. She thought it was strange that she liked this place so much.

Hearing nothing, she cracked the door and seeing an empty hallway, she made her way quickly and as quietly as possible to the throne room.

She walked in as though she had not just

whisked herself into the Lair without invitation and was greeted by the King's son, Mathew.

"Miss Applebee! What a nice surprise!" he said as he stood from a corner desk Verity had never noticed before. He took her hand and bowed graciously.

"Becoming quite the diplomat, aren't you?" Verity teased. Mathew grinned. For a long time, Verity had not been sure if it would classify as a smile but having lived with the Goblin's for many months, she knew now they were not actually contemplating eating her innards but really were just smiling.

"I told you she'd come," a low grumble came from across the large room. Recognizing the voice did not stop Verity's heart from trying to break her ribcage. In a panic she moved behind Mathew.

Mathew turned a large black eye on her.

"I thought you said you were surprised," Verity whispered.

Mathew shrugged. "I was. I have learned not to believe everything I am told. I will have to learn to trust my gut more."

Verity sighed.

"I'm not here to hurt you," Duran said as he came to a stop in front of them.

"What *do* you want?" Verity queried.

Duran reached out and Verity backed up a step even though Mathew was standing ground in front of her.

"What *is* going on?" Mathew asked.

Duran took in a deep breath and glanced at the ceiling before addressing Mathew. "I need the girls help so that I can save Lerina and get on with my life."

Verity's eyes narrowed. "So, you're not here to take me back to your mother? Who I should mention, I'm pretty sure was going to kill me!"

Duran clenched his jaw and gave her a dark look which must have been hard with vibrant purple eyes. "Look, Mother has her own agenda. I was present for dinner and nothing more. Her game is her game. I don't care. I just want Lerina and I think you can wake her." He paused and lowered his head, but his eyes bore into Verity's. "I will owe you a great debt if you pull it off."

Verity raised her head at that admission and appraised Duran. He seemed bent, haggard even.

"I'm tired," he said. "I'm tired of these games."

Verity nodded and put a hand on Mathew's arm. "I think it's okay, Mathew. I would like to try to help her."

Mathew looked at Verity thoughtfully before patting her hand with his own large hairy palm and moved away so that he was no longer between them.

"I insist you join us for dinner before you go," Mathew said, making Verity smile.

"I would love that," she answered. "I'm starving."

Seeing everyone - King, the Queen, and the twins was a balm to Verity's heart. Such love and tenderness from such an unusual family. Duran brooded during the entire meal and was the only darkness attending the feast. The Queen kept patting his arm and he would roll his eyes.

Verity's lips quirked periodically as she came to the conclusion that this lovely family had taken on the dark knight of the Fae as a friend and he loved them as much as she.

"How will we do this without your mother finding out?"

"You mean your Aunty?" Duran said drolly. Verity paused to give the family connection some thought, and not for the first time either.

"Duran is your cousin?" The Queen asked, the shock on her face making both Verity and Duran share a chuckle.

Verity snorted and gave several quick nods in succession.

"That is correct, oh lovely Goblin Queen," Duran groveled.

The Queen leaned over and whacked him on the arm. "Did not see that coming," she commented as she stuffed a fork of withered green something into her mouth.

"We will visit Lerina. You will do your best and we will see what happens. If she wakes, you can vanish. If she does not..." Duran stopped speaking and glared at Verity.

Verity was not so new to magic or to the powers of the Fae to know exactly she was dealing with.

"Duran!" the Queen admonished. "Verity is *our* friend. *And* she's going to help you. *Willingly.* If she cannot, then you leave her be."

Closing his eyes, Duran drummed his fingers on the table as though he was counting down his anger before nodding and opening his eyes. He and the Queen had some kind of silent communication going. Verity glanced at King. He was entertaining the young ones with a fork flying through the air to their mouths. Verity smiled. The human gesture was not lost on her. King met her gaze and smiled. It was interesting that he let his wife do the royal work while he played. Verity didn't know if she would ever understand all the ways of this Goblin Lair, but she certainly did enjoy it.

"No harm will come to her by my hand," Duran said.

"Promise!" the Queen said, and Verity couldn't help but wonder about their friendship. It seemed so unusual. But if it helped her handle this situation and get out unscathed, she was not going to complain.

"I promise," Duran told her. Then he stood and held out his hand to Verity.

"Now?" she asked.

"Are you finished eating?" he questioned, a smirk quirking up the side of his mouth.

Verity sighed. "Yes."

She stood and took his hand.

The next moment she was once again kneeling at the bedside of Lerina. She looked at Duran who was standing elegantly next to the bed gazing at the woman with a lost look on his face.

"How did you do that?" Verity wanted to know. He raised an eyebrow. "Transport us, just like that?" She snapped her fingers.

He bent his head. "You mean the exact same thing you did to remove yourself from my mother's clutches?"

"Yes, but I have to concentrate and then step in to it."

Duran shook his head. "No, you don't. It's just the way you've developed it. It works with just a thought, a simple decision. The focus is important though. You wouldn't want to be distracted or change your mind mid-thought." He looked introspective. "And you don't have to step into it. You just go." He shrugged and waved gently toward the gaunt lady laying on the bed, looking very much like she would pass away at any moment.

Verity wasn't willing to let it go just yet. "But I saw you step into nothing. And others."

He sniffed in irritation. "When you know where you are going, it is convenient to be walking both when you leave one space and enter another."

Verity looked thoughtful. "Makes sense," she commented.

"I'm so glad you think so." He gestured at Lerina. "Now can we save my mate?"

FOUND

Chapter 27

"Dude, we were just about to send out the search party. Next time, bring your phone."

Andy blinked at Liam before nodding. "Yeah, sorry about that, lost track of time."

"Everyone is fed and we're packing up the trucks. Go grab your stuff so we can jam," Brick said as he tossed a duffel bag into a funny looking truck. Andy ran inside to get his bag.

After only having two driving lessons in his life, somehow he had managed to drive the jeep back in town, park it in a random shopping center parking lot and then get back in the nick of time.

Andy debated telling them about his apparent abduction by his own family. He decided the mission they were on was so important, he didn't want to distract anyone. Especially when the truth was, though their methods were unorthodox, he couldn't be happier to have found more family. He was excited to learn more about them, and to get to know his extended family much better. Once the Princess was found and everything had settled down, he would tell the Guardians, and the Queen, his story.

He changed his clothes, leaving the poorly fitted ones in the trash bin and ran outside. He hoped no one would be particularly interested in the odd weapon poking out of the top of his duffle.

The Guardians and Sloane spread between three vehicles; Dustin, Brick, Andy and Evan in one, Liam, Sloane, Simon and Sheba in another and Kam and the Siren took a two-seater. Zarra had some kin nearby they were going to visit after the mission. The caravan headed across Ireland toward the Cliffs of Mohr. Apparently, that wasn't their destination, but it was nearby. As the scenery flew by, Andy was intrigued by its beauty. One day he wanted to go exploring when he didn't have the pressure of a mission to worry about.

Andy was looking forward to stopping for lunch since he'd missed breakfast. Sloane had saved him some beans and toast which was interesting but not near enough food. He was eager to taste more of the local cuisine. Liam and some of the boys had been talking about drinking their share of Guinness while they were here. Andy hadn't tried it yet, but it didn't look all that appealing to him. Whiskey had a prettier color, but again he hadn't tasted it yet. He figured he had a long time ahead of him and could taste such things when the desire hit him, if it ever did. It wasn't like it would create any effect on him anyway. The only thing that created an intoxicating effect on gargoyles was oranges or orange juice and he had always hated them, so that was convenient. Andy was particularly leery of anything that hindered his ability to think straight.

It took over two hours to get to the other side

of the country, two hours for an early lunch and then another hour to get to the area the Queen had directed them to. Andy was still amused by the crew's camaraderie and the complete happiness that came crossed Liam's face when he took a drink of his first Guinness. Andy had fallen asleep half an hour into the trip and had slept through everything except lunch.

They drove past the location looking for a hidden place to park but the area was mostly farmland and was surprisingly flat. After some discussion, it was decided they would simply park and head to the cliff side. Rather than going through the ruins, they would go through the cave entrances and see if they could avoid some of the Raks. The goal was to get the Princess, and any other Guardians or hostages, and get out.

They parked near the road and walked over. The wind whipped around them like a lure to the cliff side. Sloane held on tight to Liam's hand as they walked, her scarf smacking Andy in the face. After the third time she grimaced at Andy and tucked the scarf in tighter. They stopped about forty feet from the edge. Sloane turned her back while the men stripped and changed. Andy tried not to notice that Zarra had no compunctions about watching everyone and seemed pleased with Kam afterward, if her smile and the lick she gave his cheek was any evidence. Andy had a fleeting thought of Charlese and grinned despite himself. He was looking forward to bonding.

As soon as he was changed, Brick ran toward and off the cliff. They waited in eerie silence as the wind gusted around them. Dustin and Evan stood together closer to the edge. Sloane pulled her jacket close while Liam put a large swirling arm around her.

"It's so quiet and desolate here," she whispered to him. "There's no noise at all with the exception of us. I can't feel anyone either. The only hues are the guardian gray and Zarra's usual rainbow cornucopia. It's weird, Liam."

Liam squeezed her closer but remained silent. Andy was familiar with his battle mode.

Brick appeared and landed nearby.

"There are three cave entrances but only two of them look used. The third is quite small and I don't see the tactical value. The other two are large enough for a gargoyle. One has a ledge," Brick pointed to the left, "and the other does not but both look traveled."

Liam nodded and walked over to Dustin and Evan, leaving Sloane beside Andy. "Brick, take Dustin, Simon and Sheba to the cave with a ledge and proceed as planned. I'll take Kam and Zarra. Evan, I'd like you to stay here and guard Sloane and Andy. I'll let you know when I need one of them."

Chapter 28

A rush of bodies down the hallway, including the guards from her doorway, caused Lauren to look up from her book. She could feel the pounding of feet through the ground, and it made her toes tingle. She placed the book on the bed and stood. She would only have one chance.

Walking slowly to the door, she allowed herself to feel her body, like putty in her capable hands. She had changed enough times now to feel mostly comfortable in her second skin. It was a scary, yet beautiful beast and she embraced it with all the love of freedom. Her body pulsed in wait for her command as she glanced out the door. Seeing her guard gone, she grabbed a small bag from beneath her sheets. It was the only thing of value to her besides life.

Heading out, she kept to the walls, careful to stay in the shadows in case anyone were to run by. A deafening cacophony of strange sounds echoed down the hall forcing Lauren to drop into a squat, eyes wide. She waited and tried to see down the dimly lit hall. The noise was monstrous, and Lauren cringed closer to the wall. A lance of fear held her frozen and when the smell of unwashed bodies tickled her nose, she wavered on which way to go.

This was not part of her plan. Her certainty wavered. Back to her room or escape? The way out was toward the noise. Lauren could stay and cower or go for freedom.

Lauren had not seen the sun nor the sky in over ten years. Though her eyes were sharp in the darkness, her skin was so pale you could make out the veins beneath. She would see the sky once more before any creature or prison brought death.

And she would do it today.

The smell was worse the closer she weaved through the tunnels to freedom. Lauren felt like she was only a turn or two away from these strange creatures. She had no idea whose side they were on and couldn't take the time to find out. If she wanted out of here, she had to weigh the odds and they were not in her favor. She held in a laugh at the idea that these smelly creatures were on their way to rescue her. If her gut was telling her straight, these creatures had more anger in one big toe than she did in her whole body. And that was saying something since being stuck here had definitely amassed a bit of anger in her heart.

The Guardians helped diffuse the anger when it was too much. She wanted nothing more than to escape and find more of them. More of what she believed was her own kind. The small mirror had given her little doubt she was a creature and she suspected the Guardians were the same. There was kindred feeling with them, something deep. There was only one way for her to find out.

Stepping into a small storage room, she dropped her bag and stripped. Lauren folded and rolled the clothes up and put them in the bag with her treasure. After tying the bag closed, she roped it around her neck and stepped into the hallway. She was flustered by her lack of clothes for only a moment before she let the change move and shape her body into a creature that would have never fit in the storage closet she had just left.

Lauren so much wanted to roar into the hall and hear the strength of her new voice but instead, she ran her fingers gently along the sides of the earthen walls. She called to the minerals and the living nature of the soil. It responded with a shiver up her arms. She and the soil had become friends in a curious way and once again Lauren marveled at herself.

She rounded the bend and saw the beasts. There wasn't a guard in sight. She reared back with a silent snarl. These creatures were not good for her health.

Pushing her desire into the soil, Lauren waited as the walls trembled for a moment before stilling. She watched in anticipation.

Chunks of soil fell to the feet of the creatures gathering in the hall. They didn't seem to notice. Lauren worried that her trick hadn't worked. She debated on giving up when her world shook. Barely keeping to her feet, she watched the ceiling ahead collapse onto the gathering mass.

Chapter 29

A loud boom shook the land and right before their eyes, the emerald green grass dropped from sight, taking Evan and Dustin with it.

Sloane screamed while Andy grabbed her arm and pulled her away from the crumbling earth.

Liam rushed over and with a glance confirmed that Sloane was okay.

"Okay?" he asked. When she nodded, he blew her a kiss and stepped to the edge of the hole. The stench of dark magic, unwashed bodies and death wafted up from the newly made rent in the Earth.

"We're fine!" Evan hollered from its depths.

"Pay attention!" Liam yelled back as he motioned to the others. He blew another kiss to Sloane. "Back soon, love," he said and jumped, leaving Andy and Sloane to wait.

He walked into the hole and disappeared into the dark rip in the earth. The rest followed leaving Andy to guard Sloane. She turned to Andy.

"I hope this goes smoothly," Sloane said. Before Andy could answer, a growl raised from the gap, tearing into the air and grabbing Sloane's heart.

"Liam," she whispered and took a step forward. Andy's grip tightened on her arm. They stood and waited.

~~*~~

Liam landed a couple of feet in front of Evan. The dust was thick. Brick must have landed just behind him and spun his tornado skills because a whoosh of heavy air swept down the hallway right before the dust was pulled from the air and dropped to the ground. Brick appeared from the miniature dervish and smiled, his white teeth sparkling in the darkness.

Liam turned back to Evan. Evan's face was smudged with dirt and he had grass in his hair. He smiled and opened his mouth to speak only nothing came out. His eyes widened as several inches of dagger pushed through his chest. Evan's hand went to his heart and his eyes met Liam's.

"I'm sorry," he coughed out before dropping to the ground.

Liam roared as a calm rage rushed his veins and before he knew what he was doing, he watched the head of the Rak fall from its neck, its dagger thumping to the ground next to Evan.

"Raks!" he shouted as more the foul-smelling creatures rushed in.

Chapter 30

Lauren watched the dust settle. She caught a glance of a creature just like herself before noticing that a couple of the beasts were still standing. One turned and met her eyes. Screeching, it jumped toward her with a long sword clutched in its hairy arm, the other two hot on its tail.

Raaak.

Lauren froze for half a second. She had no experience in a fight. Though she was bigger, their skill would win with these odds. Lauren had just made a horrible mistake. She turned and ran.

Lauren had made it around the bend before she caught herself. There was no retreat today. She would lose or she would win but she would fight for her freedom. She paused and turned as the first beast rammed into her body. He hadn't expected the full stop and she used his impact to turn herself and land on him while pushing his sword arm away and using her forehead to bash in his ugly furred face. Its body went still but the screech from behind had her turning, the sword arm still clutched in her grasp. The second creature had already jumped toward her with no way to stop himself and plummeted down to the hilt of the sword. She blinked away a rush of tears as she watched the life leave its amber eyes. A pained sound and then more screeches had Lauren scrambling up from the bodies. She wrestled the sword from the dead hand and turned to the final beast. Its face was contorted into something resembling a smile. It cocked its head and licked its lips like she was fresh steak and Lauren couldn't fight the dread as it wove its way into her limbs. She bent her knees and held out her arms, one hand clasping the sword. She had no idea what to do to gain any chance in hell at winning this fight.

But fight she would.

The beast rushed her. She held her ground. Her gut told her to run but she wanted to be free. She would get him close enough to crush or stab. Whatever means presented itself. She waited.

Lauren's mouth dropped when she watched its eyes bulge as a sword appeared poking out of its chest before wrenching further up its body and then vanishing away. The beast fell to the ground at her feet. Lauren's massive body slumped, and she caught herself from falling with a stabling hand on the wall. A cry of anguish escaped her lips just before she saw him.

The magnificent creature before her was huge, at least twice her size. His black eyes met hers and she watched recognition ripple through their depths. He dropped to a knee and bowed his head.

"My Princess," he stated, his voice deep and powerful.

Lisa Barry

Lauren's knees buckled beneath her. She crawled to him and wrapped her arms around his neck.

"You found me."

FOUND

Chapter 31

When Lauren finally registered the first words the beautiful creature had said to her, they were already walking down the hall together toward the smell of the sea. He held his sword out and kept scanning the path they walked. His skin was like her own but swirling in a way she imaged a wave or a vortex might do. She wanted to question how it worked, but was too overwhelmed.

After two turns, they started passing bodies. The smell of the beasts was even worse than before, their putrid blood filling the halls with death. It was the gaping hole in the ceiling that cleansed any empathy she might have had for them. She stopped as the ceiling ended and looked up.

"The sky," she choked out. She dropped the sword she was holding and reached up with both hands, forgetting the potential danger and instead reveling in the warmth of the sun and the cool air that whispered across her leathery skin.

Time started moving and Lauren caught hold of herself. She lowered her arms and blinked several times before turning to move once again toward the smell of the sea.

A horrible screeching came from behind and there was more coming from further down the hall. Dirt and dust kept falling from the break in the ceiling. Lauren grabbed her dropped sword from the ground and shriveled against the wall.

"Stay close," the big Guardian told her. He turned away to slash at the monsters catching up with them. Lauren glanced back and forth. They were surrounded.

Chapter 32

Lauren didn't wait to see who else might be her friend and who wasn't.

She ran. Leaving the caring Guardian behind, she dodged anything that came into her path. One of the strange fuzzy creatures was to her left. She veered closer to the wall and slipped past the sharp metal weapon that swung her way. She encountered a strange swirling wind in the tunnel that blew debris around, catching one of the monsters in its whorls but oddly never touched her. She passed a beautiful creature, another Guardian she thought, who lay unmoving on the ground. Stopping was not an option but her heart went out to him.

On she ran, kicking up dirt and dust from the floor as she went, hoping it would cover some semblance of her flight. The darkness around her became lighter. The smell of the salt water was stronger and Lauren ran even faster. She hurled herself around a bend.

Only to find no ground beneath her feet. She screeched in surprise.

As Lauren fell toward the crashing ocean below, she turned her body and looked at the greatness of sky. It was as beautiful and calming as she remembered.

Chapter 33

Andy heard the scream and rushed to the edge of the cliff, Sloane at his heels.

He looked over the edge just in time to watch a gargoyle he didn't recognize plunge into the cold water.

He pulled his jacket and shirt over his head.

"Andy!" Sloane yelled in a panic.

"It's okay," he growled, his gargoyle form already taking over. He kicked his pants to the side. "I'll be okay but get away from the edge before you fall!"

He jumped, forcing his wings to speed up the descent, and aiming for where he'd seen the gargoyle last.

"Good luck!" he heard Sloane's yell and just before he entered the water, Liam's growl reverberated throughout the caves above.

Once he was underwater, there was only a calming silence. He took a soothing breath of bubbly air and tried to see in the hazy water. He went deeper, listening and searching for any sign of the fallen gargoyle.

A school of fish raced past and he headed in the direction they had fled. Wings tucked into his body, he used all the force he could muster to chase the trail of bubbles. When Andy finally saw the gargoyle, a thrill raced through his nerves, a kindred recognition he would have scoffed at if someone had told him before now.

This was no normal guardian.

Adrenalin aided his rush to her. When their eyes met, the gargoyle lifted a hand toward him but stopped mid-motion.

Andy reached her then, scooping her up and turning toward the surface at the same time. He raced upward in long strides and burst through the waves and into the sky.

Chapter 34

Lauren found herself coughing and gasping for air while a heavy wind tore around her. She was momentarily distracted by wondering why she didn't feel cold before another rack of coughs had her spitting out salt water. She opened her eyes to find a lady sitting next her, a smile on her lovely face. A lady! Lauren hadn't seen another female besides the witch since her capture.

"Hey, there, Princess," the lady said. "I'm Sloane." She pointed to a gargoyle hovering next to her and blocking the sun. "And this here is Andy. He's the one who pulled you out of the water. That was quite a fall."

Lauren smiled and sat up, surprised to feel the weight of the bag hanging around her neck. Her body was winded but recovering quickly.

"I'm Lauren," she replied, and her smile took over her face, exposing her fangs. Still on her knees, she stretched out her arms and breathed in the dust free air.

"How wonderful it feels to be out of there." Lauren dropped her arms. "But I've got to go back. I have to save them!"

She stood quickly but Sloane held out a hand. "Hang on, Princess. Let's wait for the all-clear. I would get my ass handed to me if you went in there while they were still taking down the Raks."

Lauren nodded and they all moved to the hole in the ground and looked down. Grunts, screeches, and growls echoed down the hall and into the late afternoon sky.

Minutes trickled by slowly as the three stood staring into the darkness.

"No!"

The holler echoed around them. Eyes wide, Sloane turned to Andy. He shrugged.

"I think it was Kam."

Sloane pressed her lips together and looked up to the sky. Lauren felt a rush of guilt.

A rush of noisy activity came from below and a gargoyle flew up from the hole holding a woman. He handed the lady...Lauren frowned. It wasn't completely a lady but an odd lady creature. She watched Andy take the lady gently and that's when she noticed the green sludge that appeared to be leaking from her side. The Guardian, Kam she presumed, raced to a pile of clothes on the ground. He pulled a plastic bag out of the jeans pocket and pushed all the clothes into it before sealing it. There was a rope attached and he pulled it over his head.

He went back to Andy and took the lady.

"I'm taking her into the ocean, the water will heal her. They're almost done down there. See you all later," he said and then turned away, jumped into the air and dipped out of sight cliff side.

The sound of a machine broke the silence. It

rumbled closer. Lauren snuck a look at the metal in the distant sky before glancing back to the hole. They stood awkwardly for several minutes before Lauren spoke.

"I'm sorry about your friends," she mumbled. An arm wound its way around her torso and Lauren found Sloane giving her a side hug, which would have been funny with Lauren being so much larger right then, but only felt warm and forgiving.

"It's not your fault, Princess. None of this craziness is your fault."

Lauren closed her eyes and swallowed hard to hold back the relief she felt. The tension in her shoulders eased a bit.

"Andy!" A voice bellowed from the hole.

"Yes, sir!"

"You can bring me my wife now, please."

Sloane laughed.

Andy snorted. "Right away, sir."

He held out each of arms and looked at Sloane and then Lauren.

"Ladies?"

Lauren held onto Andy's left arm while Sloane wrapped an arm around his waist, and he wrapped his around her so she wouldn't fall. They jumped.

Her breath caught when Lauren met the gazes of the group standing in the hallway of what had only hours ago been her prison. There were four like her, at least that she could see crammed into the small space, big brutes with whorls moving along their skin and one...she struggled for a moment. Lion? Was that a lion? The catlike creature, it's jaws and nails far more pronounced than the pictures she had seen, leaned against one of the Guardians, which Lauren knew without doubt, was what they were.

Sloane rushed to one of the Guardians. The half dirt covered tuft of red hair on his horned head seemed out of place.

"I'm fine," he said and embraced her. Another Guardian rushed forward. She recognized him as the one she had first met, who had saved her.

The Guardian bowed before her while Andy made his way to the group and started shaking hands.

"What's your full name, Princess?" the Guardian at her side whispered. Lauren looked up at him and smiled before glancing back to the crowd before her.

"Lauren Griffin."

"Everyone," he announced, "I am pleased to present you with Princess Lauren Griffin."

"Oh, I'm no Prin...," Lauren started to say but was cut off by the sight of one of the Guardians. It was Andy. He moved toward her from behind the crowd of bodies but not *around* them. He somehow walked *through* the bodies until he was in front of them all. His skin changed from a misty translucence to the smooth hard skin she expected and recognized. He bowed before her and then lifted his head to meet her eyes.

"My name is Andrew Chamberlain and I will

be your personal Guardian from this moment forward."

An audible gasp came from several of the other Guardians.

Lauren's heart pounded in her chest. "Oh, please, there's no..."

Once more she stopped. Bright strings of rose-colored light burst from her chest at the same time strings of ice blue shot from the guardian in front of her. They stood and watched as the strings intertwined and joined before disappearing with a flash. Lauren clutched her chest and was shocked to feel his surprise and fear pulsing as though it was her own emotion. The Guardian, Andy, with what she presumed was panic on his face, met the eyes of the large guardian beside her whose mouth peeled into a large grin.

"Don't worry, Andy. This is not the same type of bond that you are thinking of."

Lauren felt more than saw the fear in Andy's heart subside before he bowed once more and went to lodge himself into the small space open at her left.

"Congratulations, Andy," one of the guardians in the crowd offered.

"I don't think so," came a gruff voice behind her. Lauren knew before turning who it was. She quickly stepped backward and turned to meet Marten head on. A dagger hung in the air, frozen. It was headed in the direction of Andy, but Lauren's movement had it plunging toward her head.

"Marten?" she squeaked. He was not the Marten she was accustomed to. This Marten was a Guardian. His leathery skin roiled just as much as the other Guardians standing nearby. His horns were slightly underwhelming she thought but his teeth were fierce. Lauren could not be more surprised if the dirt ceiling above was raining roses.

"Let them go, Marten, just kill me and get it over with, " she said, her voice stronger this time.

"No!" Andrew shouted and moved forward.

Lauren flung out a hand. "I will lose no more Guardians from this game you are playing, Marten. I have had enough."

"You leave me no choice, El. I cannot let them have you."

"Make *me* your choice."

"ENOUGH!"

The growled word echoed throughout the halls. Chunks of dirt and roots fell from the hard-packed walls hitting the ground with thuds throughout the tunnel system.

Marten drew up into his full height and glared. "This is not your concern, *Helen*."

The largest Guardian of them all pushed through and stood before him. If Lauren had not heard the feminine undertone in the voice, she would have never known that another female had joined them.

"I tried to stop her," a male's voice whispered as he rushed up behind the behemoth of a Guardian. Lauren watched as the female Guardian moved up next to her. She snatched the dagger from Marten's hand. He just stared at her. Lauren didn't know if it was in denial, respect, or maybe even chagrin.

She had little time to ponder on it as the female Guardian beside her shot her leg out so fast Lauren barely saw the motion before Marten was flying backward. He landed hard and before he could move to get up, another Guardian materialized from the shadows. The snap of bone echoed around the cave. It was followed by the squelch of a dagger parting flesh.

An intake of surprised breath was the only other noise in the hall. Lauren thought it was Sloane.

Lauren wanted to look away but forced herself to watch. The dagger thunked to the ground. Marten didn't move again. The Guardian kneeling at Marten's head stood and came forward only to kneel again in front of the huge Guardian beside her, his tuft of red hair a lone color in the cave.

"I am sorry, my Queen."

The Queen said nothing but placed one clawed hand on the Guardian's head while brushing tears from her face with the other.

FOUND

Chapter 35

When the Queen had regained her decorum, she turned to Lauren and took her hands into her own. Even though she felt safe, Lauren was scared by the sheer size and power emanating from her.

"Hello, Princess," the Guardian Queen said. Lauren couldn't help but smile. It was such a ludicrous thing for them to keep calling her. It occurred to her, this Guardian must be experiencing so much pain right now. She squeezed her hands just before the lady Guardian let hers go. The man behind her stepped up and took one of the lady's hands in his own.

The Guardian with the red hair was standing now and Lauren watched Sloane touch his arm delicately. He pulled her to him and despite their current size difference, tried to bury his face in her long hair. Sloane closed her eyes and held him close for a moment before addressing her.

"Princess, this is my husband, Liam."

"Nice to meet you," Lauren said trying to be polite in this surreal moment of her life.

Liam gestured to the lady Guardian. "This is our Queen, Helen Barrows. And beside her is her husband and our Director, Joseph Barrows."

Lauren made an awkward curtsy, and

someone laughed. There was no mistaking Helen Barrows for what she was, a true Queen.

The friendly Guardian, the one she had met first, sidled up to her and dipped his head. "I'm Brick."

Lauren laughed. "Good to meet you! Thank you for helping me earlier."

The Guardian with the lion waved from the group. "I'm Simon and this here's Sheba." He pointed at the Lion who chuffed at her. Lauren waved.

Sloane pointed to a Guardian hanging back. "That's Dustin," she said. The Guardian smiled and waved.

"Truthfully," Sloane told her, "we're going to have to do this all over again once they're shifted."

Lauren looked at each them. "Maybe not." She was fairly certain the sound of each of them, their scent, and the way they held themselves would give her the clues she needed to tell them apart.

If nothing else, there were the strings of energy that emanated from each of them. She felt them living and breathing, bound to her solidly, a part of her inner being. Her heart would tell her what she needed to know. The strands were a curious thing, they felt too personal right now and she wanted to keep that to herself for the moment.

Introductions done, the Queen made her way to the Guardian on the ground and unmoving. She crouched over her son, her husband, Joseph at her side. The group moved down the hall to give them privacy and encouraged Lauren to show them the prison she'd called home. Lauren wasted no time and ran to the nearest trapped Guardian. There were six at any one time and due to their life span and toughness, they lasted a long time. But not forever.

The first one she encountered was sleeping. Lauren placed a hand on his shoulder.

"Carson?"

His eyes shuttered open. He smiled.

"What's up, El?" She kissed him on the cheek as she pulled the needle from his arm. He tried to grab her arm.

"El, that…"

He stopped when the Guardians came into view. He squeezed his lips together and leaned his head back into the wall, letting out an emotional moan.

"We're saved," he whispered as he was unstrapped from the chair and helped to stand. Brick pulled the man into a bear hug.

"Good to see you again, my friend."

Lauren left them behind to find the next one. And then the next. They were all in varying states of weakness with only one unable to stand. They had barely gotten to him in time but with nourishment and rest, Brick, the name of the first Guardian she had met, thought he would make it just fine.

There was one thing left to do and then Lauren was happy to leave this place forever.

She walked into the room and looked around for the last time. It had always scared her. The chair. The podium with the single bowl.

The Witch.

She hung limply from chains in the ceiling. Feeling bold, Lauren moved to her, wondering if she even lived. She stared at the wrinkled, deathly pale skin and watched for any sign of life. In recent years the woman had aged dramatically. Lauren had a vague memory of a different Witch from some time before but this one had been with her for so long the other Witch was a faded and almost unseen dream of the past.

The faintest of breathes caused a motion in the Witch's chest. Lauren stepped back and ran to the door.

"In here! We need water!"

Moments later, Liam and Sloane appeared with a few bottles from the storage area. Liam quickly disabled the chains and rested the Witch's body on the ground. She moaned but otherwise did not move.

Sloane moved to her and went down on a knee with an open bottle of water. She let a few drops touch the Witch's lips while Liam sniffed the bowl. He scowled.

"They must have mixed the Witch's blood with the Princess's for some type of spell."

"And the Guardian's blood." Lauren pointed to the rows of tubes coming in at the ceiling and hanging high above over the bowl. "It was how they hid me," she offered.

Liam nodded his head and gave an impressed grunt. He took the bowl and hurled it to the other end of the room. It shattered and fell almost soundlessly to the dirt floor.

FOUND

The Witch's eyes cracked open as Sloane's dripped more water to her lips. Cracks of bloody lines opened on her lips when her eyes founds Sloane above her.

"Liam!" Brick yelled from the doorway.

"Finally," the Witch croaked out as her arm came up and settled on Sloane's forehead.

Sloane's body went stiff as the witch breathed in heavily.

Liam struck the witch's arm, the snap of bone causing a pitiful wail. A glance at her showed skin already starting to smooth, her hair became glossy and her eyes were sharp. Despite the broken arm, she pushed away from them all, scuttled to the wall and slowly stood.

Sloane had fallen over, Liam catching her. She looked at least fifteen years older and her breathing was labored.

"What did you do?" Liam demanded. The Witch looked sheepish.

"My apologies," the Witch said. "I was starving."

"Well, fix her!" Brick's thick voice echoed in the room.

"It would likely kill me," the Witch whispered.

"Don't worry, Liam," the Queen said as she entered the room. She was a sight to see in her gargoyle skin, dwarfing even Brick. She leaned down and squeezed Liam's shoulder.

"We shall find a way to restore her. I have just the coven in mind."

The witch's brow quirked up. The Queen met her eyes.

"Are you Evanora?"

The witch pulled her head back in surprise. "How do you know me?"

Helen gave a sad smile. "We got word a few years ago the Swiss coven master's bride, a powerful green witch, had gone missing." She shrugged. "It made sense. How was Marten able to hold you?"

The witch glanced around the room but made no move to relax her alert stance. Lauren could tell she was sad by what happened, and her fear of the Witch lowered a notch.

"He drugged me. Something nasty and powerful. When he took to the sky, I couldn't fight him without access to the earth's energy."

She waved her unbroken arm and the roots in the walls and ceiling around them reached out and then entwined together before hanging in an artful fashion. "Before he landed, he told me about the fire power he had. He pointed out where he kept it. There in Switzerland, only a few kilometers from my home. He said…"

Pain washed over her face. "He told me he wouldn't waste any time blowing up my entire coven if I did anything less than what he asked of me. When we landed, he showed me around and then contained me in this very room. I would never hurt my family. My sacrifice continued their life."

"Spoken like a green witch, Evanora. We will cause you no harm and will get you home to everyone in one piece."

"But he…"

"He is dead and can no longer harm anyone," the Queen stated and then left the room.

Lauren stared at the empty doorway. Her heart broke for the Queen's loss, but she was free now and there was absolutely nothing in the world that could stop her from feeling the restrictions in her life fall to the ground with a resounding boom.

Chapter 36

Verity's heart leapt. The great Duran had feelings after all. He covered them well. She glanced at him. The desperation he must be experiencing melted any hang ups Verity had about helping him. Even the fact that he had kidnapped her. Since meeting him and learning so much, Verity felt almost comfortable in her skin, certainly more confident.

She sat carefully on the bed and looked over the lady called Lerina. When Verity had first seen her, she seemed so young and lifeless, just a girl hanging on to the threads of life. But now, looking closer, perhaps feeling more with her new senses, the girl seemed old. Her skin was dry, and Verity almost watched for it to flake off from the bones it clung to. She shivered.

"Stop procrastinating," Duran scolded. Verity glared.

"Can you wait outside?" she asked.

"No."

"Then at least sit in the corner so I can concentrate without you breathing down my neck."

He rose and backed away. Verity turned back to her patient. She pulled the covers away from

Lerina and was surprised to see that despite her long sleep, she had been well taken care of. She was clean, smelled faintly of daisies and wore a ridiculously soft night gown. Verity made a mental note to find out later where to get one for herself.

Lerina's face held no peace. It was thin and slack yet the calm you see in a person's face while they are sleeping was absent. Verity remembered the last time she had put hands on the woman and a jolt of adrenalin shot through her nerves in anticipation of the pain. Her heart sped up a bit and she tried her best to pretend the fear wasn't stealing its way into her muscles and bones.

If ever she was challenged, this would be it. If she could do this, she could do anything. The Fae Queen herself could not undue this mess. Verity frowned. No one had actually told her that. The Queen was a strange woman and who could really say what she would or wouldn't do in any situation. Verity was certainly in a mystery as to what to expect from her *Aunt*. The word, yet to be spoken out loud, felt odd in her mind. The Aunts she had grown up with were much more predictable. A laugh gurgled at the back of Verity's throat and she realized anxiety was holding her still.

There was only one way through this. She reached out and touched Lerina's face. It helped to know someone cared for the sallow creature. Even if it was just Duran. The skin was cool but not cold. There didn't seem to be a breath, but Verity could feel life, faint in the space before her.

Closing her eyes, Verity sat then and just felt the space around her. She felt for the now familiar sweetness of magic. She felt for the energetic hum of life, for the soft murmur of the small things you can't see and for the...

Verity's eyes flew open. She glanced back at Duran, but he hadn't moved. He simply raised his brows at her. She looked back at Lerina and she too was the same, with no motion, not even a faint sigh or quirk of the lips. But Verity had felt something. It had been, it was...

Not wanting to close her eyes again, Verity licked her lips and took in a deep cleansing breath then slowly let it out.

It was anger. No...fury.

Verity had the sinking feeling the spell holding Lerina in this horrible state was a killer. It scared Verity to the bone. Duran would suffer no loss in Verity's life if something happened to her. She needed strength.

Hopping up from the bed, Verity held out both hands. In one appeared a bar of chocolate and in the other was a cup of orange juice. Two things to give her a ton of quickly usable energy. It wouldn't last long and that was fine. If she made it through this, she would eat a nice steak for dinner later to make up for it.

Duran didn't budge from his chair in the corner. He simply waited patiently, like there was nothing in the world that needed immediate attention.

FOUND

The trickle of fear started down her spine again and right next to it was the zing of sugar. She shook out her hands and went back to the bed. This time she climbed on it and knelt. She wanted to be able to use force if she needed to.

Without allowing herself to think about it anymore, Verity placed her hands on Lerina's shoulder, her thumbs resting just under her clavicle. She closed her eyes and it took only a moment to locate the spell. The anger. Just feeling the periphery of the spell, Verity knew it was placed above the girl's heart. A wave of grief passed over her and she pulled it away. She could not grieve for a loss that was not true. She was in this to win. Fear buzzed behind her ears, like the chuff of a demon.

Blowing air slowly out of her lips, Verity lowered her right hand just slightly. She felt no heartbeat, but the rage pumped in its place, tendrils of violence lanced at her hands. There was only one way Verity could think of to battle such a heated, irrational thing.

Pulling herself up a bit, Verity pulled the magic from herself and channeled it into both her hands as she rested them over Lerina's heart.

She shoved.

The magic streamed from her hands, attacking the temper with speed and force. Verity fleetingly wondered who would win this fight.

As though it had heard, pain, like a thousand shards of metal, shot into her hands. Tears rolled down her face as she pushed back, holding her hands in place while trying to untie each of the strings of chaos from the lady's withered body. The tormenting stabs changed then to a soothing caress that left Verity almost faint with relief.

It attacked again with teeth. Shredding her skin, and pulling at bones.

Verity whimpered but held on, keeping her eyes squeezed closed. She was almost depleted of the sugar energy she had inhaled and hoped her own life force would be enough.

Her own life force.

Verity realized two things. It was just a spell. It had no true purpose of its own to win. It was a trap, triggered to display its ire but there was no emotion in its existence, just a shade of someone's evil power.

Verity had the true purpose to win.

There was one other thing. Something she had in spades.

Love.

She added her secret ingredient to the rush of magic, and shot it into the spell of ire.

The Fury hiccupped and Verity thought she'd won for a split second before it continued its brute force anger. It was fighting hard. Verity fought back but she was tiring.

The Fury stopped then and instead began to wrap itself close to Lerina's heart, filling in gaps and squeezing arteries.

It was going to try and kill. Verity panicked. Her magic started to ebb and flow, pulsing like a blender full of rocks. She pulled away. A sob choked her, and tears dripped down her face.

A whisper fluttered through her mind. Verity

instinctively reached upward and felt the magic. The Fae realm was filled with it. Verity abruptly understood she could take it. The whisper faded away as Verity willed the smooth and excitable essence of the world in through her skin. It pooled and throbbed and screamed its joy in her blood. Verity felt it pounding against her ears, her bones. She shook her head from its heavy weight and finally threw her hands on top of Lerina and forced the joyful magic into the girl like a shot of adrenaline.

Lerina screamed.

Verity could feel Lerina's agony, but she kept forcing magic into her. Warmth was seeping into Lerina's body, filling her with life and it gave Verity hope.

Faintly she heard Duran yell. She opened her eyes and at first glance, she wanted to throw up her hands and give up while she was still alive. Lerina was nothing but a pile of dust covering the bed. The lovely night gown was in tatters below her. Duran was howling now and if she didn't work fast, he was likely to kill her.

"It's a trick!" Verity hollered into the storm that roared in her head. Her hands still pushed glowing magic into a body she could not see. "She's still alive!"

His voice faded and just when Verity thought she would collapse, the spell exploded.

Verity was tossed from the bed to land awkwardly on her side. She felt the crunch of bone in her hip, a stab of white pain and then darkness.

Chapter 37

In her human form and dressed, Lauren stood barefoot in the luxurious grass of County Clare, Ireland. It was cloudy and though it was starting to dip into the horizon, the sun still touched her, and her skin sucked up vitamins it had not known in years. Her surroundings were bigger and more beautiful than any book or description she had read.

Gripping her bag at her side, she smiled. Wherever they might be, she hoped her parents were okay and wondered if maybe they could be proud of her. In her bag rested the handful of pictures she had of them, carefully guarded with cardboard and wrapped in plastic.

Wiping away a tear, she searched the sky for the strange mechanical sound. She found it coming in from the water side. The flying vehicle came whirring closer and landed far enough away that it was not as frightening as it might have been. A helicopter. The queen had arrived in the one she had observed earlier. She had no recollection of seeing one before today. And she was going to ride in one!

The Guardians were still in their gargoyle form. She had a name now for the creature that lived within her. The fact it was daylight and monsters were roaming the hills did not seem to bother anyone. The land held so much magic and it was hidden from human eyes.

The air was cool and crisp, and she gulped it in, just in case this was only a dream.

They were going to drop off Sloane before continuing on to who knows where. Lauren prayed for the lady even though the Queen said it would be simple to cure. Lauren was also pleased the witch, Evanora, would be returned to her family. That lady had earned a notch of respect from Lauren. She hoped one day they could visit again but definitely in a better place.

Lauren was a *Princess*. She had not expected that. The Guardians were not precisely a kingdom, but the structure worked. The Queen, Helen, told her she was free to do whatever she wanted with her life. Because of the efforts they had gone through to get to her, Lauren knew she must be important. It must strain the Queen to offer her any options except the one of Princess.

She didn't need time to think about it though. She looked at Andy. He stood speaking with the man from the helicopter, concern etching his face. He was attached somehow to Sloane, who was being loaded onto the machine with her very angry, very demanding husband. Lauren looked forward to having a man growl that much for her one day.

Then there was Andy, her own personal guardian. She wasn't sure what it meant yet but for now, it was a comforting thought.

Lauren had a family and a future more incredible than she ever imagined.

She was home.

FOUND

Chapter 38

They stood at the yawning hole looking down into the darkness that was once Lauren's home. Nine of them gathered in silence, the Queen, Joseph, Andy, Brick, Liam, Dustin, Simon, Sheba and Lauren. Sloane was unconscious in the helicopter that now stood quiet while they gathered.

The Queen started to speak.

"Today we gather for many reasons. One, we witness the close of a long battle with someone who was once dear to my heart. I will always have the memory of his smile when his soul was pure." She cut off a sob and paused to collect herself.

"Two, and most important, we mourn the loss of many brethren. Whether a son, a friend. There are too many warriors to list now who were lost during this battle but here, on this location, we remember Evan, Tio and Connor.

"Evan was a kind and generous soul. He thought nothing of himself when someone was in need." She looked at everyone with a small smile.

"With a dedication to detail and a love of the stars, Tio might be on a space station or beyond had he not answered the calling of his blood. He always said that flying was close enough." Brick chuckled and nodded.

"And Connor. His need to ever be the better warrior kept him moving, always looking for the next thrill. His loss brought us future."

"Their dedication was never doubted and never waned. They did many of us a service by being our friend and we will miss them all dearly.

"Death may seem a silent darkness but in turn it can bring light and completion of one life so that another may begin.

"I know that when we see them again, we will be greeted with a stronger bond than ever."

"Be free, Evan. Tio. Connor. We look forward to having your company once again."

Helen took Joseph's hand and silently let the tears fall.

Dustin, who had been close with Evan, stood sobbing as Liam put a comforting arm around his shoulders. Simon and Sheba held back as neither of them knew Evan. Brick and Andy stood together solemnly.

Lauren had her own task to finish and she knew there was something else she could do to help. She looked to the Queen who nodded.

Moving to the opposite side of the hole, Lauren held out her hands in a flourish. She began to sing, a song she remembered well, though she couldn't remember how or from where, and she started to play the earth like a symphony.

The sorrowful group watched as their Princess mended the rent in the land and sang a hymn of love lost and peace found.

FOUND

Chapter 39

To avoid being seen, Kam had found the west face of the nearest island and stood in the shallows of a small cove so his love could rejuvenate her energy and heal in the salty ocean.

Once she was healed, they waited for the cover of darkness before continuing to their next destination. Kam scooped up the Siren who had stolen his heart and jumped into the air. It felt good to use his wings but even better to hold this gal in his arms. Zarra, better known as Jaws, purred into his neck, sending shivers down his spine. He smiled, feeling the pull of his skin against the scar that disfigured it.

Jaws herself was a scarred and secretive warrior but no matter, his beast and her beast blended like the magic that tied them together.

Kam had received his scar before his first change. He'd been only eleven years old when he caught someone hurting his mother. She'd not made it through the experience, and he had almost lost as well.

For the next five years he had wondered every day why he had been allowed to live. He was no warrior then. He was no one. A kid on the streets, trying to survive and not even knowing what drove him to keep going. Those were days he looked back on now as character building. Dark, scary days with bursts of sunshine through cracks of hope.

He had helped others without homes. Finding cardboard, finding food and sharing it. He remembered feeding the cats and the dogs before himself and rolled his eyes at his soft heart. Thank goodness his friend Ryan had found him after his first confused shape shift, just skin and bones.

Kam blinked away the moisture in his eyes when he thought of Ryan. He had lost his life to one of the terrible weapons that had been developed specifically to kill their kind, to kill a creature with impenetrable skin.

Kam course corrected his flight to avoid a low flying plane. Wouldn't be good to be seen as the monster in the sky after avoiding such things for so long. A long, long time since his childhood.

Ryan had become his best friend. After finishing school, Kam had been posted with Ryan and he had never looked back. It was Ryan who had been helping the Siren's without Kam knowing. Kam wondered if it was because he was afraid Kam would bond with one of the Sirens and become temporarily insane, leaving his friend at the curb or if it was because he was doing the very thing Kam used to do as a child, a giving hand that was not logical but needed to be done anyway. Kam chuckled. He'd never know but he appreciated the irony.

Jaws lifted her head and met his gaze. She put a gentle hand on his scarred cheek and gave him a rare smile. He would die for this woman. The unbidden thought settled something inside him. A fear for her safety or something deeper perhaps. He knew logically she was perfectly capable of protecting herself, better even than some of the monsters he knew. It hadn't changed his paranoia but now, his nerves finally fell into a calm place.

He wondered if Jaws had felt it through their bond. She shifted and set a soft kiss on his shoulder. Then she licked him and laughed. Evil laugh. He chuckled and shook his head.

He starting to drop toward the ocean, they were close to their destination. Jaws turned in his arms, so he held her waist only, her face scanning the ocean for her island.

The Island of Sirens.

Her body started to change as he held her. It was a treat for Kam as she generally hid her true form. She knew he cared not what she looked like. He had learned long ago it was the inside that made a person, not the flimsy exterior.

Her hair had a living quality about it normally but this close to the ocean, it blossomed and grew into a tangled and breathing thing. Kam squeezed her waist. He liked every form she took. When they had first met, she had tried to scare him with her true form. Milky white eyes, jagged shark-like teeth and bluish skin. She glanced at him in her native form and smirked.

Dropping even lower, Kam searched for the familiar cloud cover and a lump in the middle that would be a floating island. The Sirens could stay hidden thanks to their magic, even though it was fading these days due to technology.

Another fifteen minutes passed before he saw it. He veered down and just before hitting the water, he dropped Jaws in and watched her dive gracefully from his arms and into its depths. He skimmed the surface in a lazy circle until she leapt from the ocean and back into his arms.

Jaws had wanted to revitalize just before meeting her kin again. This area had not been visited by her in a very long time. These kin were different from her close family in the Bermuda triangle. These kin were rough, and warrior fit. The Scots of the Siren world. Jaws had wanted her magic refueled and her mind clear before meeting them once more.

Spiking straight up to the island in the sky, Kam came up from the bottom only veering at the last moment to come around its side and land noisily into the first clearing he saw.

He released Jaws and they both stood, arms out, ready for anything. In moments, twelve warriors surrounded them. Each held out a weapon and a hand prepared to use magic.

"Greetings," Jaws said and then growled, her hair twisting and turning around her head. One of the Sirens coked her head in recognition. She lowered her weapon and took a step forward.

Jaws felt safe to continue. "I have come to visit my kin. To see how you fare and offer assistance in this new world of technology and death."

Some of the Sirens nodded in agreement and welcome but a few only narrowed their eyes.

"I care not," Jaws said, "if you want the

assistance or not, only that you survive. We in Bermuda have learned ways around the changes and are starting to procreate once more."

A couple of the Sirens chins moved slightly up in interest.

"I am with child." Jaws pointed at her abdomen. "Strength will reign once again in our numbers."

Kam blinked and replayed what Jaws had said. Then he replayed it again. Before he could move from his frozen shock, a Siren with a doubtful look on her face stepped forward.

"I would hear your thoughts on this matter, though I am doubtful. We have been losing our battle with this new world for too long."

Jaws nodded. "I know exactly what you mean but it can be turned around. We can adjust to the new world, and not just survive but survive well. There is much change ahead of us, but we are not the only creature changing to fit. We can do this."

Kam could stand it no longer. He put a hand on Jaws shoulder. She met his gaze.

"It is true?" he asked her. "You are with child?"

"Yes, why would I lie?" She shrugged. Kam stood straighter and pulled the kaleidoscope of emotion into a safe place in his mind, deciding not to ruin her endeavor to help these people. He would wait until later to set her straight.

He stood by, as a guard he supposed though he knew he wasn't needed. The Sirens had taken to Jaws' rough and tough demeanor and settled in to hear what she had to say. They were hungry for answers and most listened with an open mind.

Kam knew some would have a very hard time changing from their flesh-eating ways and he wondered if Jaws would allow it to continue. Cannibals, the lot of Sirens once were, but things changed. He was glad of that. He didn't think it would sit well with him if his bond had chosen a mate for him that liked to chomp on human bones. It would be difficult indeed.

He couldn't help but flinch when he thought of her cold shoulder about their child. Had she taken him to try to continue her species? Or was she in it like him, for the long haul? He shoved back the nervousness and heartbreak until he knew the truth.

After two hours, they decided to break for rest. He and Jaws were led to a hut and left with a basket of fruit and a raw bone. Kam didn't look too closely. He didn't want to know what creature it had come from.

As soon as they were in the hut, Jaws grabbed the bone and started digging in the sand. She wrinkled her nose at him. "Deep sea creature, nasty things," she said. "My kin are as desperate as I suspected."

Kam changed his form and sat on the straw bed.

"Zarra?" he asked softly. He rarely used her name and she knew it. She paused in patting the sand smooth and then stood and sat before him. She took his hands.

"I did not know for sure until the ocean filled me once more with life. I suspected, but it is not the same as knowing."

"I'm going to be a father."

Jaws scrutinized his face. "You will not be leaving now?"

He frowned. "Why would I do that?"

"Many men leave when their female's become swollen with child. It is difficult to grow them and keep the..." She waved at her face. "Façade of beauty."

Kam exhaled loudly. He leaned in and took Jaws' face in his hands.

"You are my mate, my bonded," he told her quietly, "my love. You are *always* beautiful to me."

"But I thought..."

"I am not the norm, silly." He tucked her hair behind her ear and watched it twist out again in defiance. "I will be here, and I will raise this child to know both its parents. We will do this together."

Kam watched his hard and battle-weary mate blink away salty tears.

"My world changes mysteriously again," she finally said. "I think I might enjoy this one."

Kam scooped her up into his arms and hugged her. He didn't let go for a very long time.

~~***~~

Chapter 40

Andy stood on the Bridge and gazed down into the foggy blue water. It was a calm evening and the waves rippled rather than crashed below him. He could almost feel the answering flap of the gills hidden in his neck. It was still strange, but it brought him even closer to them. On the return from Ireland, he asked Brick to stay with the Princess so he could stop and see the lake where he had lost his parents.

A soft hand slid into his. He knew who it was without looking. He smiled despite his momentary melancholy and squeezed. There were so many odd things in this incredible world he had stumbled into and he loved it.

"I only have a few minutes," Charlese whispered, trying not to interrupt his moment. Andy released her hand and instead slipped it around her shoulder and pulled her close to his side. Her nearness settled him.

"They would be proud of you, you know," she said, resting her head on his chest. She wasn't tall enough to reach his shoulder.

"I know," he answered as he ran his fingers up and down her arm. "I miss them so much. But now I have a new family. The legacy my father has left me, well it's…"

"I know," she answered without letting him finish. "And then there's *my* family."

A deep chuckle from his chest shook her head. She laughed and hit him in the stomach.

"It's going to be fun," he teased.

"It's going to be crazy," she added.

"It's going to be an adventure," they spoke in unison and watched the sun dip from the sky.

~~***~~

Chapter 41

Liam held Sloane's soft hand in his as they walked through the park. Darkness was imminent, so most of the people were leaving which gave them some peace alone. A breeze lifted the leaves in a whispered song while the birds randomly greeted one another. A strange group of animals had started to follow them along the trail. Liam smiled as he cast a sideways glance at Sloane.

She had melted the cold from his heart.

The sight of the Witch draining her essence had almost broken him. He had been more scared than anything he'd ever experienced in his entire life. Thanks to the Queen's goodwill, the Fae in Switzerland gave them a formal introduction to the coven of able witches in their backyard. The Coven Master was overjoyed to see the broken witch and grudgingly healed Sloane in exchange for being forgotten once more.

Liam brought Sloane's hand to his mouth and breathed in her scent as he left a soft kiss behind. Her responding smile made his heart glow.

"Mine," he whispered.

Sloane stopped and put her free hand to his jaw. He knew she could see his raw emotions swirling around him like a tornado. She pulled her hand from his and slipped her arms around his waist, pulling him close and settling her head into his neck. He wrapped her in his arms and with the leaves fanning the trees and the delicate scent of wild flowers nearby, they stood together.

Liam pulled back and kissed his wife deeply. She melted into him, their bond dancing with joy.

Then they linked hands once more and continued down the trail.

~~***~~

Chapter 42

Verity opened her eyes to see Duran sitting in a chair next to her. She was tucked into a soft bed from the way she felt, and her hip had been healed though it was still sore. Thank goodness for healers. She smiled. Duran smiled back and for once he looked happy.

"Where are we?" she asked.

"One of my homes," Duran said.

"Must you be so obtuse?"

Duran only smiled wider.

"How long have I been out?"

"Three days."

Verity felt her jaw drop and pushed it close. "Wow."

"You needed some recovery time."

"Apparently." Verity moaned and moved to sit up. Everything ached. Duran handed her a glass of water and she drained it before handing it back. She blinked a few times before remembering why she had ended up healing on a bed. She swung her head around to ask him when a lovely lady walked into the room holding a tray.

Gone was the gray skin, the sunken cheeks, and the dull blond hair. Standing before Verity was a beautiful Fae, glowing and healthy with sparks of gold magic popping around her. Lerina beamed at her before setting the tray down on the side table.

"I am so glad you're finally awake so I can properly thank you." Lerina's voice was light and airy like a spring breeze. "I've made you many things from Earth since I didn't know which you liked. I hope you're hungry."

Verity eyed the tray and was impressed by the pile of pancakes, a bowl of onion soup, brightly colored salad and bread slathered with butter. It was an odd mixture, but Verity was starving, and she liked every single thing laid out on the tray.

"I *am* hungry and that looks amazing," Verity said as she sat up straighter. Lerina placed the tray over Verity's knee and then sat on the bed, grinning like a child.

"Please eat and let me know if it is okay." Lerina blushed. "I enjoy cooking and have dabbled in many different customs. Earth food is odd but fun."

Verity couldn't help but laugh as she forked pancake into her mouth. It was soft, and just sweet enough with a hint of vanilla. She eyed Lerina who raised her brows and nodded eagerly. Verity chuckled to herself and swallowed.

"Delicious," she said.

Lerina clapped. "I cannot thank you enough for what you have done for me." She paused and glanced at Duran who stared at her with adoration shining in his eyes. "I was aware of everything. I heard every word, watched every move and could do nothing."

Verity's heart squeezed at the thought of such horror.

"He thought he would never get me back, and I thought I would never die, that he would move on and I would never live again. Never know him again." A tear trickled down her face and it was the only evidence of the hardship she had endured. Verity reached out and took her hand. Lerina gave it a squeeze. "Even worse," she continued, "I almost killed you on the spot once I was able to move again."

Duran cleared his throat. Verity frowned, "Why?"

"Because I thought you were her at first."

"Who?"

"Why Isla, of course."

Verity glanced at Duran. He looked solemn. "Your mother," he divulged.

"Ohh," Verity sighed. "That makes sense."

"Not really," Duran disagreed, "seeing as how we thought she was dead and all."

"And why wouldn't she be?"

"Because she hit me with that furor spell," Lerina said in such a way that indicated Verity should know these things.

"Still not getting it," Verity replied, the spoon in her hand still while she waited for clarification.

Duran leaned forward. "Some spells get life from their maker. Other spells come from or are held by *things*. Fury comes from its source. If what Lerina says is true..."

"It *is*," Lerina interrupted. Duran's lips quirked slightly but he continued.

"The spell's magic should have died with your mother."

Verity leaned her head back against the wall and looked at the ceiling.

"This just keeps on getting better and better."

Once Verity had healed enough, it occurred to her she was probably in danger. Duran swore that his mother was a cunning woman but only reverted to killing when she was feeling threatened.

"And what about my mother?" Verity asked as she put on her shoes. Duran and Lerina sat on the bed and watched her.

"You can run forever or just go live. She will find you if she's able, or if she wants to. And if she doesn't," he shrugged, "better for you."

"She might try to find you," Lerina added. "She's different from our current Queen. Not better or worse, just not the same."

Verity struggled not to frown at the useless message Lerina had divulged. The fact she was still alive and had been in Fae territory for over four hours with no sign of the Queen made her more apt to believe Duran.

She gave them both a regal curtsy and hightailed it out of there.

Verity went home. She revived her dead plants, cleaned her apartment (even though she had fleetingly thought she might be able to magic the dirt away, she decided the exercise was more important), took her car for a drive to the grocery store and slept in her own bed.

Her place may not be much, but it was hers and she was comfortable there. Verity sat at her small two seat dining table and perused the online job ads while she sipped a cup of coffee.

A sniffling sound brought her straight up in her chair. Her ears strained to listen. Something warm pressed into her thigh followed by a long sigh.

Verity slowly looked down and met the pleading red eyes of the Vigilo. Bringing a hand to its furry green head, she gave it a scratch. The Vigilo closed its eyes and relaxed against her.

Smiling, Verity continued to scratch her new pet's head.

She scrolled through the nursing jobs absently, not overly impressed with the selection, when an ad for medical positions in disaster zones made her pause. She clicked the link.

Medically trained persons needed for planetary disaster recovery relief. Dangerous environments are a given. Travel required. Interested parties must sign waiver. Complete form for more information.

Verity completed the form, attached her nursing certificate, and clicked apply. Then she leaned back in her chair, scratched her Vigilo behind the ears and smiled.

~~***~~

FOUND

Chapter 43

Helen sat on her couch at home, her husband cradling her hand.

She smiled fondly at Lauren, her protege who was chatting amicably with Andy about the merits of poker versus spades while they put together a tray of tea and cookies. That had been their request, not hers.

They brought the tea and treats into the room and placed it on the table before the Queen. They sat in chairs opposite, Andy tossing a cookie into his mouth as Lauren sat serenely and smiled at her new guardians.

"I want you all to know," Lauren glanced at Andy before meeting the Queen's eyes once more, "there is no question in my mind I'm where I need to be."

"I am so pleased to hear that," Helen said. She had lost a son but gained a daughter. Helen would never understand why her son had turned against his heritage, but she knew without a doubt the girl in front of her would run with the torch and protect this lot of rebellious creatures with every power she had.

Joseph squeezed her hand. The touch said everything.

Lisa Barry

All was as it should be.

FOUND

Epilogue

King waved to Drog, his first in command before turning the corner toward his quarters.

As he walked down the halls of the Goblin Lair, he ran a finger along the ground and smiled to himself. The earthy smells, the familiar walls, they had given him so much these last few hundred years. He was ready to walk away from it all to be a full-time father and husband.

Soon.

He entered the nursery and found his human wife, Hulia, sitting on the floor, watching their twins wrestle a few feet away. She was waif-like, and her hair was so light it always moved like there was a breeze. It was one of the things that had endeared her to him. Her feisty nature resided in a small but extraordinarily resilient package. He sank down next to her and took her hand. She leaned in for a light kiss before setting her golden smile on him. He couldn't help but beam back.

A shriek from their daughter, Skiyandra, brought his head up. She was standing next to her brother, Carl, and pointing, the devil in her eyes, with triumph. King laughed.

"Oh," his wife said, "a package came while you

were with Drog. It smells very strange."

King sniffed the air and frowned. She was right. There was an odd scent of pine and fur. He licked his lips. Whatever it was, it smelled tasty. She pushed a cloth covered box toward him. King frowned again as he pulled it in front of him.

He lifted the cloth and found himself looking at a small hairy brown creature. It looked back at him with black beady eyes and grunted.

Hulia picked up a white card that had fluttered to the floor and opened it.

"Most Honorable King and Queen,
I wanted to show you my gratitude for your kindness and encouragement during my stay at your home. I learned so much. I cannot ever repay you, but I hope you and your family will enjoy this gift with my heartfelt thanks. I know you always wanted to see a guinea pig, and now you have one to call your own.
Sincerely,
Verity Applebaum"

Hulia laughed. The King smiled and sat a little straighter.

"It is an excellent gift," King said, his eyes crinkling at the sides as he looked at his wife. "Do you eat it raw?"

His wife snorted. "You're not supposed to eat them at all."

"But it smells delicious," he complained, his shoulders lowering a fraction.

Hulia shrugged. "Humans have them as pets."

FOUND

King grunted and watched as his daughter caught sight of the odd little creature in the cage. She scuttled over and tried to get a clawed hand between the metal bars. The guinea pig made small squeaking sounds and pushed to the other side of the enclosure. Not to be left alone, Carl rushed over to the other side and jabbed a finger through the bars. He started to cry, and his mother scooped him up. The guinea pig was squeaking madly while darting around the cage in terror.

"I don't think it's going to do too well with our family," King said.

"I think you might be right," his lovely wife agreed. "It's more dinner than a pet."

"More like a snack," King muttered and lifted Skiyandra into his arms as he stood. He held out a hand for his wife, who still held Carl and they headed off to dinner.

Later that evening, Hulia went to the nursery to remove the guinea pig and stash it away until she could decide what to do with it. The door hung open and the cage was quiet and empty. A glance around the room told her it was gone.

She shook her head and headed back to her rooms, glad the King hadn't offered to share his snack.

~~*~~THE END~~*~~

A Note from Lisa

Would you like to receive a free short story about the Origins of The Guardians? Just tell me where to send it!

Follow this link: http://tinyurl.com/LbarryFreeBk

I hope you enjoyed this trilogy as much as I loved writing it. If you did, please leave a review, it helps so much!

I love hearing from my readers, feel free to reach out!

Email: LB@authorlisabarry.com
www.AuthorLisaBarry.com
facebook.com/authorlisabarry
instagram.com/authorlisabarry/

About Me

From the age of five, I grew up in Florida which I quickly found was not a good enough reason to avoid wearing black. A daily color choice, I constantly pine for weather cool enough to wear boots but I generally just stay locked indoors. :)

I live with my incredibly supportive (and hot) husband and amazingly awesome kidlets. I count it a blessing that they still love me despite the deafening sound of my music muse throughout the house.

Writing and reading every minute I can, I count on the many gargoyles who listen carefully when I read to them aloud. As you might have guessed, I collect gargoyles and books. I also LOVE to travel (always planning my next trip to Ireland!) and enjoy time with friends and family.

Lisa Barry

Also by Lisa

The Gargoyles Den series

Origins
The Guardians
Rogue
Found

<u>*Ruby Dust*</u>, a stand-alone short story

Ghirn, sheriff of Ruby Dust on Mars, catches an outlaw, saves a couple of humans from cannibalistic Dearndins and calms the ladies of The Pink House. All in a day's work.

More book info:

<u>http://www.authorlisabarry.com/books/</u>

Thank you for reading!

www.ingramcontent.com/pod-product-compliance
Lightning Source LLC
Chambersburg PA
CBHW050402030726
47503CB00006B/1986